Everyone Who's Anyone

A **Starlet** Novel

Everyone Who's Anyone

A **Starlet** Novel

by Randi Reisfeld

Hyperion Paperbacks
New York

Text copyright © 2007 by Randi Reisfeld

All rights reserved. Published by Hyperion Paperbacks for Children, an imprint of Disney Book Group. No part of this book may be reproduced or transmitted in any form or by any means, electronic or mechanical, including photocopying, recording, or by any information storage and retrieval system, without written permission from the publisher. For information address Hyperion Paperbacks for Children, 114 Fifth Avenue, New York, New York 10011-5690.

First Edition

1 3 5 7 9 10 8 6 4 2

Printed in the United States of America

This book is set in ITC Century Light.

Library of Congress Cataloging-in-Publication Data on file

ISBN-13: 978-14231-0502-2

ISBN-10: 1-4231-0502-8

Visit www.hyperionteens.com

Everyone Who's Anyone

A **Starlet** Novel

Chapter One

Doin' It Up Malibu Style!

WHAT: It's a wrap! You are cordially invited to join Jacey Chandliss and costars for a Splash-Down Party, in honor of the completion of her newest movie, *Galaxy Rangers.*

WHERE: The Polaroid Beach House, Malibu

WHEN: August 5, cocktails at 5 p.m.; last dance at . . . ??

WHO'LL BE THERE: Everyone who's anyone. This means you!

BYO: Bikini, beach towel, biceps, booty and boobs

Barefoot and bikinied, seventeen-year-old Jacey Chandliss scampered up a rocky rise in the dunes along the

Malibu beach. The biggest party of the summer was in full force just below her. She needed a moment to savor the amazing scene of which she was now officially a part.

Jacey tipped her chin skyward and inhaled the salty ocean air. There was something wonderful about the sea breeze, even though it played frizz-o-havoc with her thick copper-colored hair. She took off her D&G aviator shades and placed them, tiara-like, atop her head.

To her left, the late afternoon sun sparkled on the wide expanse of the Pacific Ocean.

To her right, a three-story, pink stucco beach house sat on the sand. It was hers! Well, at least for the month of August: Jacey and her friends had decamped from their Hollywood house to live it up in a real-life Malibu McCrib.

How strange and surreal was that?

Wait, it got better.

A *People* magazine–issue's worth of "Sexiest Young Hollywood Stars" were right under her nose, dancing, noshing, playing kickball, and mingling. They were the tan, the toned, the tabloid-bait—celebrities known by their first names only: from *A* for Ashlee (as in Simpson) to *Z* for Zac, from *High School Musical*.

"A celebrity petting zoo," her friend Dash called it.

Dashiell Walker was the boy next door from back home in Michigan. He was Jacey's closest male friend, one of three BFFs who'd come out west with her to kick off her acting career. The other two were Desiree (Desi) Paczki and Jacey's twenty-one-year-old cousin, Ivy Langhorne. The posse, they jokingly called themselves. Starlet was what they called Jacey.

Right now, Dash, Desi, and Ivy were mixing it up at the Splash-Down party, hobnobbing with the stars, plus everyone else who'd been part of *Galaxy Rangers*. Over a hundred people had shown up for the party. Jacey had learned that even the richest stars couldn't resist free food, an open bar, and the chance to bask in the glory of being among their own: the young, hip, famous, and fabulous!

Most amazing of all? Every single celeb was there because Jacey Lyn Chandliss, a once ordinary wannabe actress from Bloomfield Hills, Michigan, had invited them. Put it this way: a year ago, the closest she'd ever come to the Hollywood star species was when she'd read about them in magazines. Now, thanks to winning TV's *Generation Next: The Search for America's Top Young Actor*—like *American Idol*, but for acting—she *was* them. A movie star!

"Earth to Jacey! Come in, Jacey!"

She spun around, nearly losing her footing.

"What's it like on *your* planet?" A male voice teased. Okay, how long had curly-haired Dash been standing there, with two frozen margaritas and a smile?

Jacey blushed. "I was taking a moment."

"A moment contemplating how lonely it is at the top?" Dash asked dramatically.

"Lonely?" She tossed her head regally, taking a drink from him. "*Shirley*, you jest!"

"Is Shirley here, too?" Dash pretended to look around.

They burst out laughing and clinked glasses.

Blue-eyed, whip-smart Dash had taken to life on the "left coast" like Paris Hilton to a camera. Jacey was still amazed by his lightning-fast assimilation.

When had the former conservo-nerd morphed into an L.A. hipster? These days, Dash was all aviator shades, skinny jeans, and snakeskin sandals. Only his "George Clooney for President" T-shirt belied his true—that is, former—self.

Everything in Los Angeles was different from back home in Michigan. Out here the vibe was casual entitlement; the views breathtaking; the values—twisted. To say the least.

"I came to escort you back to the hoi polloi, Mistress of Malibu. Your presence is requested," Dash told her.

"By who, specifically?" She hoped this summons came from Matt Canseco, the actor-slash-person-of-*most*-interest to her.

"Not Matt. He's not here yet." Dash knew her so well!

"Then who?"

Dash's cell phone rang. "I've got her, Cinnamon," he said into the teeny phone. "Yeah, I know *he's* on his way. We'll be right there."

Cinnamon was Cinnamon T. Jones, Jacey's agent. Jacey couldn't even guess who "he" was.

Dash flipped his phone closed and enlightened her. "It's the Big Guy—as in Landsman. Currently en route to our party."

Jacey tensed. Guy Landsman was the head of the movie studio that was releasing *Galaxy Rangers*, which made him Jacey's boss. Cinnamon had insisted on inviting him, but had assured everyone that he was far too important to actually show up.

"What a buzz kill," Jacey mumbled, following Dash down the dunes. "Who needs their boss at a party?"

"Adjust your attitude, Princess Persnickety. Inside word says that Mr. Boss Guy is about to drop the F-bomb."

"When did you start speaking in tongues?" Jacey asked. "What's the F-bomb?"

"You'll see."

Back down on the beach, Jacey threaded her way around fluffy beach towels, discarded flip-flops, and designer totes. Their owners were busy massaging each other's egos—gushing, hugging, back-slapping, tossing flowing tresses, and flexing muscled biceps.

Ice clinked in people's glasses and, in some cases, through their veins. True, everyone here was a "someone," but *not* everyone was to be trusted.

As if on cue, a pair of conjoined blonds accosted Jacey.

Slinky Sierra Tucson and fake-baked Kate Summers, both in floppy hats and bling-ringed bikinis, had costarred with Jacey in *Four Sisters*. They'd become fast frenemies—pretend friends. Only, they'd dispensed with the pretend part months ago.

"The caliber of celebrities here is *muy* impressive," said Sierra, sipping a wine spritzer.

"For you, she means," Kate clarified, downing a tequila shooter. "But then again, you never know who might show up at a wrap party—it's not like anyone can afford to miss it."

"Sure," Dash pretended to agree. "You never know if a director like Stanley Kubrick will show up at this soiree, scouting a star for his next opus."

"Stanley Kubrick is here?" Kate, dumb as nails, shaded her eyes and raised herself on pedicured tiptoes to look around. "Which one is he?"

Jacey and Dash guffawed at her cluelessness.

"I think he's dead, Kate. They're just teasing you," the

somewhat better informed Sierra said. "But that *is* Scarlett over there."

Kate turned to stare. "Oooh, and isn't that Stavros rubbing sunscreen on Lindsay's back?" she asked.

"Maybe Stav brought some fresh Greek shipping scions along," Dash suggested. "Go forth and frolic, you two. You might get lucky!"

"What's a scion?" Kate asked, as Sierra pulled her away.

Dash's phone rang. Cinnamon again. "Landsman's limo is about a mile away. We should be on the deck when he gets here. C'mon."

"Wait," Jacey stopped him. "I'm not taking a meeting with an old exec while I'm wearing a bikini. Too high of an 'ick' factor."

Dash pulled off his T-shirt. "Here, cover your distracting curves."

As Jacey and Dash made their way toward the beach house, they got "what up?" waves from Justin and love-ya air kisses from Jessica and Ashlee, who were grazing on finger food from nearby Nobu. The priciest sushi place on the planet had catered the party.

Jacey kept her eyes peeled for the dark and dreamy Matt Canseco, but he didn't seem to be there.

Meanwhile, Dash propelled her forward, as other

guests tried to waylay her. Jacey's costar in *Galaxy Rangers*, Adam Pratt, planted himself in their path. Adam, a Ken doll in Rocawear, was sweaty from playing beach kickball. He leaned in for a smooch, but Dash intercepted.

"She's got a meeting," he explained, "Kissy-kissy after."

"Meeting—with who?" Adam said suspiciously. The young up-and-coming actor hated being left out of anything.

Jacey brushed the question aside. "Relax, it's nothing. I'll catch up with you later."

Just then, the movie's director, Emory Farber, waddled over, sweating profusely and breathing hard. "Hi star-hostess, how goes it? Word has it Landsman's on the way."

Word! Jacey chuckled. It would never *not* astound her that the Hollywood grapevine was faster than a speeding IM. Keeping anything on the down-low, was totally NGH: never gonna happen.

"Maybe Landsman is making an appearance here to announce a sequel!" Adam piped up optimistically. "That'd be sweet! But . . ." His forehead crunched. "Doesn't he want to meet with all of us? Unless . . . not everyone's in the sequel?"

Dash hurried Jacey away, leaving Adam to his insecurities, and Emory to quell them.

Cinnamon came flying off the deck, waving excitedly at Jacy and Dash. The sleekly coiffed über-agent attempted to run toward them while wearing skinny-wedged Gucci espadrilles—and sank lopsidedly into the sand.

"We've got news! It's fabulous!" she called, recovering nicely.

To upbeat Cinnamon, nearly everything was *fabulous*—a word she evoked often when she was excited.

"Hey, Cinn, great to see you," Jacey said as she held up her face for the typical *mmmwah-mmmwah* air kiss. "What do you think of the party?"

"It's about to get better," Cinnamon declared, linking her arm through Jacey's and guiding her up the steps of the polished wood deck.

Jacey's publicist, the brilliant Peyton Spinner, was on the deck, greeting their guest, Guy Landsman, who had managed to look hip *and* important at the same time. Maybe it was the white linen suit over the black Prada T-shirt, with sockless lizard loafers. And the gazillion-dollar Rolex on his wrist.

"Here she is, the girl of the hour," Guy said, opening his arms to encircle her. He and Jacey then executed the kind of no-touch embrace that only happens in Hollywood.

"Mr. Landsman—" she began warmly.

"Mr. Landsman? That's my father. I'm just Guy." He smiled, and his teeth nearly blinded her—they were so white you could read by them at night.

"It's so cool that you could come to the wrap party, Guy."

"Wait until I tell you *why* I'm here. That's the really cool part." He winked at her and sipped a tall drink that Peyton had placed in his hand.

"Guy has exciting news for us," said Cinnamon, who was nearly jiggling with excitement.

Guy pinned Jacey with his ice-blue eyes. "I keep hearing all these wonderful things about you. Your talent, hard work, and your commitment to *Galaxy Rangers*. I already think of you as part of the Avalon Studios family."

Jacey offered a tentative smile. She had nothing against him, but family? She'd never met the dude before today. She hoped the "F-bomb" didn't mean "family."

"Jacey loved doing *Galaxy Rangers*," said Cinnamon, giving Jacey a little elbow nudge. "We all believe in it."

"The whole Internet crowd is buzzing about it!" Guy crowed. "We expect nothing less than a huge opening weekend."

"The studios can predict how a movie will do based on what the fans are saying," Peyton noted.

"What *are* they saying?" Dash asked.

"Four words," Guy replied. "*Spider-Man. X-Men. Matrix.*"

Jacey's face tightened, despite the fact that Guy's word count was off. Those blockbusters had lived up to their Internet fans' excitement. But *Galaxy Rangers*? It was a fun, futuristic, sci-fi extravaganza about teams of teens who patrol the universe. No way was it the next *Spider-Man*.

"We're going to leak a scene or two on the fan site, galaxyrangersthemovie.com, to whet their appetites, toss 'em a few bits at a time. Then we'll do a music video to keep feeding the frenzy." Guy sounded as if he were describing crazed sharks instead of potential fans.

"But I didn't schlep all the way out to Malibu just to tell you that," added Guy. His eyes were now shining with glee.

"There's more!" Cinnamon said eagerly.

"Jacey, can I be completely honest with you?" asked Guy, leaning in across the table.

Something tells me you could not be completely honest with your priest, minister, rabbi, or imam, Jacey thought. But she still pulled off an interested look. "Please."

Dash kicked her under the table.

"Franchise." Guy settled back in his chair and clasped

his hands behind his head. So that was the F-bomb. Which meant . . . what, exactly?

Cinnamon beamed at Jacey. Peyton's eyes twinkled.

Dash kicked her again. She was supposed to react.

"Franchise." She tried the word out. It sounded like "french fries," and she almost started to laugh. *You want franchise with that?*

"Isn't that *fabulous*?" Cinnamon's voice went up an octave.

"You mean, sequels, like *Galaxy Rangers II*," Jacey guessed. Had Adam been right?

"Oh, no, *much*, much bigger than that!" Guy replied, leaning back in his chair.

"Prequels? And then sequels?" She tried again.

Guy guffawed and slapped the table—his Rolex made a pinging noise on the aluminum surface. "See, *this* is what we love about you, Jacey! Your innocence. Your girl-next-door sweetness! When we combine that with your Q-score, your talent, your built-in audience from *Generation Next*, your adorable looks, that's what we'll package! Without that political T-shirt, of course. That will have to go."

Jacey froze. They wanted to package her? Like frozen peas?

"The studio has such faith in you. They chose you!"

Cinnamon squealed, her eyes shining with tears.

"We believe in you, Jacey," said Guy. He was a snapshot of faux sincerity.

If he'd only stopped there Jacey might not have freaked out.

"We believe that you're a hot little commodity. You're the starlet of the moment. We are committed to making sure your moment never ends, to building you, helping you achieve the kind of long-lasting career you deserve. We want to invest in you—you, Jacey Chandliss—move *you* to the next level. We foresee a Jacey video game, a clothing line, a fragrance. You're the franchise." A triumphant smile seized Guy's face.

Cinnamon glowed to the point of radioactivity.

"I don't know what to say." Jacey stammered, her face registering panic.

"Thank you!" Cinnamon blurted. "This is the most *fabulous* news ever! And Guy came all the way here to tell you *in person*. The ultimate compliment."

"In the spirit of our new relationship, I'm here to offer you a *very* rich three-picture deal." Guy smiled with satisfaction. "Very rich. Just to demonstrate our commitment."

So that was it. He had come with boatloads of money. To buy her. He'd detonated the famous F-bomb.

"What kinds of movies would I be making?" she managed timorously.

"Blockbusters!" Guy bellowed.

"With all due respect, what kinds of roles?" Dash inquired. Cinnamon instantly shot him an "overstep much?" look.

"Girl superheroes," Guy declared, as if he'd just invented the concept. "*That's* the next big thing. Jacey could play Wonder Woman! Supergirl! Bionic Woman!"

"Anything but Catwoman," Dash joked, referring to Halle Berry's movie super-oops.

If looks could clobber, both Cinnamon and Guy would've pummeled Dash unconscious.

"Comic-book characters?" Jacey interpreted.

"Big spotlight roles!" Guy said expansively, opening his arms as if to embrace all of Malibu. "You'll be our girl, the face of Avalon Studios."

"Like Mickey Mouse is the face of Disney? A mascot?" Dash asked, scratching his head.

Jacey pictured herself with mouse ears—and almost lost it.

"She'd love it!" Cinnamon shrieked, giving Dash the evil eye.

"She'd love . . . to consider it." Dash spoke for Jacey.

"What an opportunity!" Cinnamon exclaimed, and rose

to hug Guy. "We can't tell you how grateful we are." She leaned over and draped her arm around Jacey's shoulders. But Cinnamon's attempt at making a comforting gesture failed miserably. "We're just a little overwhelmed right now," Cinn said, noticing Jacey's expression.

"Overwhelmed" was oversimplifying things. The scrawl running across Jacey's mind was: *I'm a commodity. They want to package me. I'll spend the rest of my life in tight costumes memorizing comic-book dialogue. I won't have a life, I'll have a Q-score. I'll be a billionaire. I'll be Mickey Mouse.*

She turned and made a beeline for the ocean. She didn't stop running until she was completely submerged in the warm water. She swam and swam, taking long, sure strokes. She'd gotten pretty far out by the time she realized another swimmer was following in her wake. She thought it was Dash.

Before she could break the surface to confirm her impression, he was right next to her—his arm around her waist, turning her around to face him. Jacey was about to say she wanted to be left alone, but then she found herself staring into the intense, bittersweet-chocolate eyes of Matt Canseco.

I'm Back

The "blog" days of August are here, and, lucky for us, the Jacey Chandliss diva express keeps rolling right along. Welcome back to your secret source for all things Jacey: I'm your friendly blog buddy. Whenever there's news about the starlet we made famous by voting her America's Top Young Actress, you can count on reading it right here. You can also count on no one knowing who I am—Jacey and her friends still haven't figured it out. Isn't that tasty?!

Today's update: If the reason Jacey packed up and took her posse to Malibu was to get away from us, girlfriend's got another think coming. The beaches of Malibu are public property. And that means that anyone—paparazzi, chopperazi, and pals—can sneak a snapshot anytime. Even when she's cozying up in a "private cove" with . . . he's *baaaack* . . . Matt "bad boy" Canseco!

Chapter Two

The Secluded Cove

"Who are we hiding from?" Matt asked, the corners of his mouth curving up mischievously.

Matt had arrived just in time to see Jacey's mad dash into the ocean. After catching up with her, he spirited her away to a sandy cove just around the shoreline corner from the party. Jacey and Matt could hear the festivities, but were hidden by a tall natural rock formation, so they couldn't see anyone. Nor be seen.

"I'm not hiding," Jacey protested, hugging herself. She still had Dash's T-shirt on. Dash's now-wet T-shirt. Clinging to her tight bikini.

"I don't believe you." Matt eyed her curiously, then dropped down onto the sand.

Jacey arranged herself next to him, drawing her knees to her chest.

"Cutting out on your own party doesn't look so good," Matt said as he leaned back on the sand, arms stretched above his head.

Jacey didn't know where she could safely focus her eyes. She couldn't look at his face (she'd melt), nor his smooth, tan chest. His soaked, clingy Nautica trunks were out (not going there!). So his taut, ropy biceps were all that was left to look at. She stared at the droplets of water on them, already starting to evaporate in the early evening sun.

"The big guy must have said something to send you running," Matt prompted. "It couldn't be bad news. He sends lackeys for that."

"You're good, Canseco," Jacey conceded, lying down on the soft sand. She was acutely, painfully aware of how close their bodies were.

She'd first known Matt Canseco by reputation only—a hard-partying danger boy and, in her opinion, the most talented actor of his generation. She'd gotten to know him in person the day he rescued her from a mob of lunging paparazzi. They'd been friends ever since. Platonically, mostly.

She'd fought her feelings, her instant crazy-mad

attraction to him. First, because, at the time, she had still been with Logan Finnerty, her boyfriend from back home. Then, after that ended, because Matt told her he was "too old" for her, "didn't do commitment," and, "wasn't interested" in her. "Not that way."

A trifecta of excuses, none of which Jacey believed. 'Cause, even though he had told her how it was, his body language often went off script.

He rolled over on his side, musing, "The only thing that brings the mountain to Mohammed is a bribe—Guy Landsman probably made you some big, sweet-ass offer."

"You heard?" Jacey was stunned.

"Didn't have to. I could figure it out. He wouldn't show otherwise."

Jacey turned her head to gaze into Matt's compassionate eyes.

Then she spilled her guts.

"I should be pumped, grateful—I should be celebrating. I should feel like Julia Roberts at the end of *Pretty Woman*."

"But you don't feel that way."

"Like my agent always says, millions of girls would die to be offered a launchpad to fame and fortune. And after only one movie! *Galaxy Rangers* hasn't still even come out yet; it could still totally flop. . . ." She trailed off.

"They're taking a huge chance betting on me. This is what I always wanted, right?"

"Sometimes you find out that what you thought you wanted isn't what you want." Matt shrugged. "Not even if it makes you a millionaire."

Was Matt mocking her? She and her friends hadn't exactly been thrifty. Their spending sprees were notorious in the blogs and tabloids.

She pursed her Cupid's-bow lips. "Being paid . . . *a lot* . . . for doing what you love, for being in Malibu?" She gestured to the beach, the bluffs, the blue water. "That's a dream come true. I'm the lucky one who's getting to live it."

"For a price," Matt pointed out. "If you accept Guy's offer, you'd be in movies he picks. It'd be like indentured servitude."

"No, I have no right to be sitting here on the sand in Malibu whining. I'm doing what I laugh at millionaire models for doing—complaining about their hard lives! It's just wrong."

"That's what you *say*, not what you feel. They dangled a sparkly carrot in front of you—you're not jumping at it. You're not even excited. You just *think* you should be."

Jacey sat upright and trained her eyes on the rolling surf. She wished she didn't take every word Matt said to heart, just because it was *him*. He made it hard for her by being so close, so understanding, and worst of all, so right. She stamped out the thought that Matt was the guy she'd always wished for—a soul mate, like Dash, only straight.

"Let's review." Matt pushed himself up on his elbows. His taut stomach rippled. He drew a line in the sand. On one side, he wrote the letter Q with a plus sign next to it. "Your Q-score is up, so studio-dude wants to pin you down."

"What's a Q-score, anyway?" In front of Matt, Jacey wasn't embarrassed to admit she didn't know.

"Some term they use to measure your popularity and your fame. The more people who know who you are *and* like you, the higher your Q-score. Like Julia Roberts, or Tom Hanks."

Jacey grinned, leaned over and drew a big A on the other side of the line. And not for A-list. "He wants to brand me, with a scarlet letter," she explained. "Property of Avalon Studios."

Matt laughed. "I get it. You'd be a marked woman."

"For which he'll pay me bundles of bucks." Under her letter A, Jacey drew a dollar sign.

Matt added letters to her sand hieroglyphics, which now spelled "$uckcess."

"Ha! That's good!" Jacey giggled. A gentle breeze came off the ocean and blew back her hair. Just around the bend, the deejay was playing "Rich Girl," by Gwen Stefani and Eve. She was snuggled in a secluded surf-side spot, writing letters in the sand with a really hot movie star. Nothing sucky about that.

Matt was twenty-one, four years older than Jacey. He'd been in showbiz since he was sixteen, so he knew the Hollywood game well. He would never play it, though, no matter how enticing the deal. He was all about small, quirky roles in movies that didn't play at the huge megaplexes. Indies, they were called. The license plate on his Dodge Viper convertible was INDISPRT.

She watched her independent-spirit guy add the letter *T* to his list. "Typecast. The T-bomb," he explained.

"You think? They said only three movies," she protested.

"Trust me, they want to take over your career. Shoehorn you into roles where you always play the sweet, clean, winsome heroine."

"Would that be the worst thing ever?" That sort of fell out of her mouth.

"Be winsome, lose some," Matt's wordplay was a warning. "Always doing the same kind of characters is not acting. For someone else, the offer would be hitting pay dirt, winning the lottery. But for you . . . ?" He trailed off, shaking his head slowly.

She was silent. She could have guessed what Matt was going to say. What she hadn't expected were his fingertips tenderly brushing up and down her arm. She shivered. If any other guy had done that, his intentions would have been clear. Nothing was clear with Matt, who suddenly withdrew the stroking hand.

"You've got raw talent, Dimples. But in Hollywood, talent often comes second to packaging."

An image of frozen peas flashed by again.

"You can choose to develop your talent," Matt continued, "stretch and grow as an actor, pick roles you're passionate about. Or—go for the money and not worry about your soul."

It was obvious what Matt thought she should do. But not so obvious to her.

"You gotta ask yourself," he pressed on, "is this the life you want? 'Cause being a real actor is all ups and downs. You lose more roles than you get. You gotta accept that, or go back to Michigan, to college, to that—whatshisname— boyfriend."

"Ex!" she exclaimed, a little too quickly and a lot too energetically.

Matt didn't take the bait.

"At least if I end up back in Michigan as a has-been," she said brightly, "the paparazzi will finally leave me alone."

"The only way you're getting a break from the 'razzi is to stop being so damned cute," he said playfully.

"Guess I'm screwed, then." She tilted her chin up slightly. He was going to flirt now, after that lecture? She'd flirt right back. She wanted to grab him and kiss him. She *really* wanted to sock him.

Matt grinned, then returned to the safety of career talk. "Now that *Galaxy*'s over, what are you doing next?"

"I haven't decided," she admitted. "Unless you count the magazine ad."

"An advertisement? Like, a public-service thing with a pink ribbon or milk mustache?"

"Not exactly."

Mischievously, Jacey drew a picture in the sand. It looked like two *U*'s joined together.

"Can I buy a vowel?" Matt couldn't decipher it.

"It's supposed to look like a butt—a tush. The ad is for Slickity Jeans. They, uh, boost your butt," Jacey said with an embarrassed laugh.

"Last time I looked, your butt didn't need any boosting," Matt said with a straight face.

Not again! His mixed messages were maddening! *Either get up off your flirt and do something—or stop teasing!* she thought.

The ad, she explained, was for a new line of jeans. The company had agreed to promote the new season of *Generation Next* if the previous year's winner—that'd be

Jacey—along with the previous year's runner-up, a comedic actress named Carlin McClusky, posed together in a full-page magazine ad.

"Butt jeans. That's not exactly gonna up your cred," he mused, forefinger pressed to his lips. "Hey, wait, I just thought of something."

"What?"

"Have you ever considered doing a play?" Matt asked.

"Like *Grease*? *High School Musical*? Or did you have something different in mind?"

"Whoa, ax the sarcasm, Jacey. I'm trying to help you here."

If you really wanted to help me . . . She couldn't help letting her mind drift . . . then quickly reeled it back in. She sighed. "Go on."

"It's just a small thing," Matt warned, "but I just read this play, and it blew me away. It's called *Fall from Grace*. It's a gritty story—I didn't know Rob had it in him to write this kind of piece."

"Rob wrote it? As in, your friend Rob O'Shay?" Jacey and her friends often hung out with Matt and his posse.

"Yup. I can picture you in the lead role. You'd kill in it."

"Matt?"

"What?"

"How is Rob's play going to help me with the big-ass

offer thing? I'm not making the connection."

Matt tilted his head and brushed an errant strand of hair out of his eyes. "Read the play. You'll figure it out."

Jacey considered. She'd done tons of plays growing up, in school and community theater. Serious dramas like *To Kill a Mockingbird*, *Inherit the Wind*, and *Our Town*. And she'd taken on more frivolous roles, too: for example, Sandy in *Grease*. She'd loved the rush of the audience's being right there, reacting; the adrenaline; knowing she couldn't do a second take. That was one reason she'd been so good on *Generation Next*. She did her best acting in front of an audience.

"What's the play about?"

Matt replied, "There's a fifteen-year-old girl with a seemingly perfect life. Until she hooks up with this really bad character, runs away from home, gets pregnant, and ends up living on the street."

"Sounds real upbeat," Jacey deadpanned. "Does she learn to love her parents, appreciate what she has?"

"Let's just say *Fall from Grace* doesn't end the way you might expect."

Matt had gone back to tracing her arm with his fingers as he talked. Jacey didn't want him to stop.

"What makes you think I'd be right for that kind of role?" Boldly, Jacey inched closer to him and brushed a forefinger across his shoulder blade.

"My gut."

As if that were an invitation, Jacey drew her fingers down across his chest, and then down further, tracing his stomach muscles.

"I think"—Matt was clearly getting distracted—"that you have the soul to understand this girl, her choices, her despair, her redemption." He moved closer.

"Maybe." She let her hand rest on his thigh.

"*Fall from Grace*," Matt said, caressing her cheek, "is a no-budget thing. If you got paid at all, it'd be next to nothing." They were so close she could feel his breath on her lips, practically taste him. She reached out gently to rake her fingers through his thick, dark, still-wet wavy hair.

"Just read it first; if it doesn't do anything for you, no harm, no foul. But if the play touches you, someplace deep inside . . ."

Their lips were touching. Matt slipped his arm around her waist and pulled her body closer to his.

"You think it will . . . ?" she murmured, closing her eyes. "Touch me. . . ."

Click! Whir! Click! Whir! The sounds of a camera forced them to pull apart and whirl around toward the intruder.

"Damn! The freakin' paparazzi!" Matt jumped up and

gave chase. Jacey's heart sank; their moment was ruined. Sighing, she dragged herself up, brushed herself off, and resigned herself to returning to the party.

She stooped down impulsively and drew a heart around their sand list.

The Canseco Canoodle

Jacey didn't waste any time hooking right back up with Matt Canseco—the boy who's broken her heart once before. Beautiful and talented she may be, but smart? Maybe not so much. I mean, really, how rude was it to skip out of her own party the second Matt decided to show up? And what a hurtful way to let her boyfriend back home, Logan Finnerty, find out he's been replaced! Or did Jacey think no one would know about her little indiscretion? Wake up and smell the digital age, starlet! The pictures are already all over the Internet.

Chapter Three

Bed, Beyotch, and Beyond

By the time Jacey managed to drag herself out of bed the next morning, her friends were already parked on the deck of the beach house. Flopped on cushy lounge chairs, quaffing mimosas and eating freshly baked croissants, Dash, Ivy, and Desi were deconstructing the previous day's party. Translation: mocking celebrities. Jacey hung back to eavesdrop, amused.

"Mischa Barton," Dash called out.

"String bean, string bikini. Boring," said Ivy, sniffing dismissively.

"Hello! I'd kill to be *that* boring!" Desi, round as a planet, declared. "Even for a day—Mischa for a day! That'd be my personal idea of heaven."

"She's a model," Ivy pointed out, "doing those Bebe ads. She should take more fashion chances in real life."

"Thank you, Nina Garcia, I'll be sure to tell her stylist," Dash quipped. "Next, Scarlett. Nothing stringy about her." Dash mimed an hourglass with his hands.

"Curvy, with class and attitude. She rocked her white one-piece." Even hypercritical Ivy gave the actress props.

"Lindsay and that new guy," Dash continued, running down his list of who-was-who-and-who-did-what-to-whom. "What are we thinking?"

"Get a room!" Ivy hooted. "They were all over each other—"

"—When she wasn't being massaged by Stavros, or sniped at by Paris's people," Desi added, brushing flaky croissant crumbs off her ample chest.

The party had been a sweet success. Everything had clicked—from the star-studded turnout to the music to the camaraderie, and, for the foodies, the incredible edibles.

"Okay, Beyoncé!" Dash got back to his list. "Are we voting for her *Dreamgirls* look, or her classic curvy?"

"You guys are bad!" Jacey interrupted. "What did you say about me?"

"You? One word—" Dash began.

"—Meal ticket!" Desi giggled.

"Those are two words, Des." Jacey flung herself into a

comfy lounge chair. "*Gravy train* is also two words, in case you're interested."

"You must've been having happy dreams, Sleeping Benefactress," Dash quipped. "It's late." He shot her a smile.

"It's the stroke of noon," Jacey volleyed back. "Besides, what important thing were you three doing besides trash-talking everyone?"

"Constructively criticizing," Ivy said, correcting her.

"Right. I can see that. Who's too skinny, who's too fat, who's flirting, who's canoodling in public—you're like the home edition of *Us Weekly*!"

"Speaking of covert canoodles . . ." Dash teased, "I almost sent for the Coast Guard when you disappeared into the waves."

"Why didn't you?" Jacey wondered how much had already gotten out.

"Don't play coy, Jace. This is us, remember?" Ivy reminded her.

"Yeah, just us—and all your friends on the Internet," Dash cut in.

Jacey frowned. "What exactly are they blogging, chatting, IM-ing about?"

"It's beyond chat." Desi displayed a bunch of pictures she'd printed off various Web sites.

"So bogus!" Jacey declared, grabbing the photos and tossing them over her shoulder.

"Pictures don't lie," Desi said. "You and Matt are busted."

"Well, they must have digitally altered them, because no lips were harmed, or even *touched*, during the filming of that episode," Jacey griped.

Three sets of eyebrows went up.

"Yet," Jacey was forced to add, "there might have been a prepucker, a near-kiss. But we'll never know, since the paparazzi, in a moment of epically bad timing, interrupted."

"What were you doing before the cameras caught you?" Ivy probed.

"Talking. Matt was trying to help me figure out what to do about Landsman's offer."

"How? By making out with you? I can see how that would help clear your mind," Ivy cracked.

"We weren't—" Jacey began.

"—Whatever you want to believe, little cousin," Ivy said breezily.

"Which reminds me," Dash said, "your agent has called fourteen times this morning. I told her you couldn't be disturbed—"

"—'Cause I'm already disturbed enough?" Jacey joked.

"Seriously, Jace—we have to deal with this," Ivy said. "Cinnamon told Guy Landsman that you ran away in the middle of the meeting because you were so overwhelmed with joy that you just got nervous; she told him that he has nothing to worry about." Ivy studied her cousin. "He doesn't, does he?"

Jacey didn't respond.

"Unless of course, Matt tried to convince you otherwise," Ivy said suspiciously.

"He didn't have to. I'm clear about the offer. I'd spend the next three years playing comic-book superhero characters," she said.

"The world needs superheroes, Jace," Desi said somberly. "Even if it's only in the movies."

Jacey looked to Dash. Surely, he understood her doubts and would stick up for her.

But Ivy was still warming up. "It's for three pictures, right? Then you're free to go on to other kinds of roles."

"You sound more like my agent than my cousin," Jacey said accusingly.

"I'll take that as a compliment," Ivy said. "Cinnamon's got a sweet job."

"They want to buy her," Dash finally said.

"Your point?" Ivy hooted. "The more money, the better! Pile it on!"

"Ives!" Jacey exclaimed. "We're not just about money. And you know that."

"I fail to see how getting paid a lot of money is a bad thing. You could go all Angelina and use it to save the world. Even your idealistic indie prince Matt Canseco has to be down with that concept."

"There's more to it," Jacey grumbled, annoyed that Ivy refused to consider her concerns. "I'd be so out there, my face would be on video games—and bed sheets!"

"You're already famous," Desi reminded her.

"Your future would be set," Ivy pointed out. "Your work could pay for a lot more than your college tuition. You could buy your parents a mansion, pay for college for your baby brother! Your family would be set for life. And all you have to do is act—which is what you do anyway. Which is why we're here."

Thanks for the soliloquy, Jacey thought. My future would be set, my fate sealed. She squirmed.

"What *did* Matt say, exactly? If you guys did any talking at all . . ." Ivy smirked.

"Matt had an interesting idea," Jacey said defensively.

"Besides the one where he jumps your bones, then dumps you?" Ivy pretended to smack her hand across her mouth. "Oops! Did I just say that out loud? My bad."

Jacey ignored her older cousin and described the play.

To her surprise, it was Dash who hit the brakes. "Wait a minute—does this play, by any chance, happen to have anything to do with someone Matt knows? Say, a friend who wrote it, maybe?"

"Your point?" Jacey asked, miffed. She'd expected support from Dash.

Dash looked pained. He'd never hurt Jacey's feelings—unless it was the only way to protect her. Oddly, he seemed to think this was one of those times. He chose his words carefully. "Aja mentioned a play Rob wrote. It's his first one, and of course, he'd love to get it staged. And even if Matt paid, it wouldn't be enough." He paused. "Unless someone famous—for instance, *you*—somehow decided to star in it."

Aja, Rob, and Emilio were Matt's posse, the guys who always had Matt's back. The guys for whom he'd do anything, the guys he'd help in any way he could. Not unlike Jacey and her crew.

"He's trying to use you, can't you see that?" Ivy, who was dating Emilio, had no compunctions about accusing Matt.

"Oh, Jace . . . I hate to say this, but it does look that way," Dash agreed.

"That doesn't automatically mean the play isn't worthy," Jacey persisted.

"It doesn't mean it is," Dash replied gently.

"Look, I haven't even read it yet," Jacey said. "How about we table this three-against-one attack . . . oops, did I say that out loud? I mean, discussion . . . until I do."

Ivy shook her head. "This is a bad move. Don't even consider it."

"Jacey's right, let's not argue about something no one's even seen yet," said Desi, rarely the voice of reason, who had somehow just found her inner Zen. "Let's go back to happy chat, where we dissect celebrities."

Jacey frowned.

"Or, how about we just chill and appreciate where we are? Come on, you guys, is this not the coolest thing ever, spending a whole month on the beach, in *Malibu*?" Desi said enthusiastically.

"Fine," Ivy snapped. "Let's kick back and enjoy."

A strained silence settled on the porch.

Then Ivy caved. "The scenery *is* mouthwatering. Just look out there," she sighed appreciatively. "I could stay here forever."

"I love the color of the water, how it goes from aqua to teal to turquoise to navy," Jacey agreed. "And the sand is so soft."

"Water? Sand? Forget that. I mean the meat—*muy* primo." Ivy licked her lips.

"The meat?" Dash asked.

"The boys. The dudes. Hotties. Stud muffins," Desi interpreted.

"Check 'em out." Ivy gestured to a pair of buff surfers jogging along the shoreline, wearing sweatbands and extra low low-rider shorts.

"Cousin Ivy!" Jacey said in a tone of mock horror. "You have a boyfriend. What's with the wandering libido?"

"I shouldn't have to suffer eye-candy deprivation just because I'm with Emilio," Ivy said defensively.

"Oh, no, we wouldn't think of depriving *you* of anything!" Dash teased.

"Looking isn't cheating," Ivy said.

"Oooh, look! How cute is that?" Desi pointed toward the ocean. A floppy-eared puppy was balancing upright on a surfboard steered by a long-haired swimmer.

"It's the amazing surfer pooch!" Dash exclaimed.

"I'm so taking a picture." Desi grabbed her cell phone camera and headed down the beach toward the water.

Ivy held up her drink. "Here's to doin' it up Malibu-style, and to us in paradise. Nothing can ruin it."

"Hi, y'all! I finally made it!" A chirpy voice came from behind them.

Jacey, Dash, and Ivy all spun around. Striding through the open French doors was a beauty they never expected to see at their beach house. She was slinky and tall, with long platinum tresses and wide blue eyes.

Malibu Barbie, in the flesh. Dragging a wheeled suitcase.

"Ca—Carlin?" Jacey stuttered, surprised.

"That's me!" Carlin McClusky, runner-up on *Generation Next*, responded with a blinding smile.

"What are you doing here?" Ivy asked, shading her eyes.

"You forgot?" Carlin batted her lashes and smiled demurely.

Dash frantically checked his Sidekick. Did Jacey have an appointment he'd forgotten to enter?

"We're doing the Slickity Jeans campaign together," Jacey said slowly, "but I thought that wasn't until next week."

"Isn't it great—I got here early!" Carlin crowed. "Can you point me to my room, so I can change? Then I'll come right back to catch up with everyone. I'll have whatever you're drinking. In fact, make it a double."

All Jacey heard was "my room." The house was amazing, but it was somewhat space-challenged. As in, it had four bedrooms; there were already four people.

"You're staying here? Who set that up?" Ivy didn't bother to hide her surprise—and annoyance.

"The folks at *Generation Next*, naturally. Jacey agreed to look after me while I'm out here. So generous!" Carlin grinned confidently, adding, "It's all in the contract."

Dash's face had panic written all over it. Meanwhile Jacey did a mental walk-through of the beach house. Where could they stash her? On a couch in the living room? Either that, or someone would have to share. Not Dash, obviously. Nor queen bee Ivy. That left her—or . . .

It was at that moment that she saw Desi, dripping wet, bounding toward them. Followed by a wet-haired hunk carrying a surfboard. And a puppy.

Jacey's Choice

To be or not to be—so many questions, so many choices, so little time to think. Turns out Jacey's been sitting on the opportunity of a lifetime! She's been offered the chance for true stardom, the chance to play superheroes in the biggest, splashiest movies of the decade. Instead of asking "How high should I jump?" she's whining and dragging her heels in the sand. And all because Matt Canseco thinks it won't be good for her soul? Jessica Alba is a superhero in *Fantastic Four*. Jacey, are you saying you're too good to do those kinds of parts? *Puh*-leez.

There's more! Jacey's got a houseguest, that cute Carlin McClusky, who came in a close second on *Generation Next*. Jacey could choose to mentor young, naive Carlin and show her the Hollywood ropes, or she could get jealous of the newcomer and act like a *de*mentor instead. Make the right choices, Jacey; that's why we sent you to Hollywood!

Chapter Four

Bottoms Up! The Slickity Jeans Photo Shoot

"Can you turn the music up?" Carlin called out, swiveling her bony booty. "This is my favorite song!"

"My Heart Will Go On," the *Titanic* anthem, was *not* Jacey's favorite, but protesting was pointless. It wasn't as if anyone was listening to her. Not a single one of the stylists, makeup artists, hairdressers, manicurists, or photographers at the Slickity Jeans shoot seemed to notice she was even there!

Carlin had somehow managed to shanghai the entire shoot.

They'd arrived at the photo studio a half hour earlier. "Don't pay any attention to me, I'm just honored to be here in Jacey's orbit!" Carlin had gushed to the staff. Of course, that drew everyone's attention right to her, and she kept it there.

The whole crew, from the highly paid makeup artist to a sought-after celebrity stylist, was charmed by her wide-eyed appreciation for everything they did. Now, Carlin clutched her heart as she warbled along to the sappy song.

Jacey was not feeling it. She didn't begrudge Carlin her moments of awe—had *she* been that different *her* first days in Hollywood?—but she *was* wishing someone would send a little love her way. Being the spokestush for Slickity Jeans was something she'd signed up for, to support *Generation Next*. It was, like, a favor. She assumed the staff would know that, and treat her accordingly.

Okay, maybe it was petty, but everyone knows that when the star arrives at a photo shoot, the first thing she gets to do is pick the background music. Jacey'd been thinking Beatles, Bruce, or Bon Jovi. A rock groove to go with a jeans ad, not this power-screeching. *"And I know that my heart will go on . . . and on . . . and on . . ."*

Usually stylists flocked around her, offering up accessories to complement the outfit, asking which designer top she wanted to wear or pulling out racks of shoes for her inspection. The hairdresser and the makeup artists— shouldn't they have been circling *her*, determining what would look best on *her*?

". . . And on . . . and on . . ."

Instead, they were posing for pictures with Carlin, answering all her questions. Part of Jacey conceded that it was sweet of them to indulge her—but the other part heard Dash's voice in her ear: *Give me a break.* Alas, Dash wasn't there. Nor was any of her posse.

None of them could make it: Dash was hanging out with Aja, Ivy had accepted Cinnamon's invitation to come to the office, and Desi was taking surfing lessons with her new surfer friend, Mike.

Cinnamon had sent her assistant, Kia—who was late—to represent her.

From what Jacey understood, the ad, which would run in all the glossy fashion magazines and on the hip Web sites, would feature Jacey looking over her shoulder, modeling a pair of Slickity Jeans.

"Watch your back—everyone else is!" was the tagline of the butt-lifting jeans. Across the bottom of the page it said, "Jeans for the next Generation," thereby plugging the new season of *Generation Next*.

The girl who'd come in second, the Justin Guarini to Jacey's Kelly Clarkson, was supposed to be posing in the background or on the sidelines. But it sure looked as if Carlin were trying to manipulate the photographer—whom she was now flirting with—into featuring her more prominently.

Or . . . wait, Jacey thought. Maybe the girl's golly-gee friendliness was as innocent as it seemed. That was what Jacey wanted to think—instead of suspecting Carlin, as Ivy did, of blatant self-promotion.

After the initial shock of Carlin's arrival, Jacey had been willing to give her the benefit of the doubt, but Dash and Ivy doubted there was any benefit in having Carlin with them.

Jacey's natural generosity overrode her friends' attitudes. She'd offered to share her room with Carlin—it was just for a week—but Desi had nixed it. "No way. It's your beach house, Jacey; you're paying for it. I'll share."

Dear Des, hardly a neatnik herself, was already regretting her generosity. Carlin was a slob. Her stuff was everywhere: all over the floor of the bedroom, the bathroom, and every available countertop.

It's temporary became Jacey's mantra. Slinky girl had no reason to stay after the shoot was over.

"Jacey! There you are. Let's start on your makeup!" An assistant ushered her to the cosmetics corner. Jacey settled into a comfy chair, facing a big, lightbulb-framed mirror. An array of eye shadows, liners, mascaras, lip colors, and blushers were laid out on the shelf in front of her. Marcia, the colorist, sized her up, trying to decide which direction to take with her.

Jacey was about to say she didn't want metallics or anything too red. But just then, Carlin cruised in, toting a tall latte. "Don't mind me, I'm just takin' it all in. Look at all this! It's like your own private Sephora."

Marcia was bending toward Jacey, applying a light berry-tint gloss to her lips.

Carlin sipped her latte. "Sure wish I had lips like yours, Jacey. They're so plump, like Angelina Jolie's. Mine are so thin; I'm gonna need lots of liner, lipstick, and gloss to bring them out."

"Have you ever thought of collagen?" Marcia straightened up, looking at Carlin.

"Is that what you use, Jacey?" Carlin asked innocently.

"Right," Jacey said drily. "I can't think of anything I'd rather do than stick needles in my face."

"Oh, snap!" Carlin chuckled. "Everyone knows you're a natural beauty." She turned to Marcia, "That's what they called her on *Generation Next*: the beauty. Me, I was the beast—the skinny comic."

"In this town," remarked Marcia, "skinny trumps beauty. Consider yourself lucky."

"That's so sweet of you to say, but it's none of my doing," the now overcaffeinated Carlin joked. "Never could gain an ounce, no matter what I stuff in my piehole."

Poor thing. Jacey was about to cue the violins.

Carlin continued to chat Marcia up. "But what about you? How long have you been a professional makeup artist? You're the first one I've met. I can barely wait for my turn in the chair!" She pointed to a row of eye shadows. "Are these what you're using on Jacey? This plum color is my favorite. Of course, my complexion is so much fairer than Jacey's; I don't know if it'd be right for her."

Marcia turned to Carlin, and considered. "I would play up your dazzling Tiffany blue eyes. Come here, let's see." And just like that, Carlin was suddenly standing between Jacey and the mirror, getting her lids daubed with something called "robin's egg blue." Carlin leaned forward toward the mirror to get a better look—which was how her ass ended up right in Jacey's face.

"I have an idea," Jacey said, rising from the makeup chair. "Why don't you work with Carlin first. I'll go over to the hairdresser."

"Are you sure?" Marcia spun around.

"Oh," Carlin burbled, "can I have false eyelashes? My eyes are my best feature and—"

Jacey quickened her pace. If Carlin craved attention that badly, let her have it, she thought. She was over it. Besides, Jacey had a lot more than jeans to think about.

Matt Canseco topped that list. Matt Canseco, last seen chasing a paparazzo off the beach; last heard from more than a week ago. No further mention, by text, e-mail, phone, or carrier pigeon, had been made of the play he'd been so hot for her to read and consider starring in.

Jacey had been obsessing about Matt and their touchy-feely beach scene all week. What was up with the tender caresses, the almost kiss? Matt *had* owned up to his attraction to her, but insisted he wasn't going to act on those feelings.

Jacey thought she'd been getting closer to changing his mind.

Was she? Or were Ivy and Dash right? Was Matt just toying with her so he could help his friend? And if that was true, where was the script? He wasn't pushing her.

Cinnamon, on the other hand, called every five seconds about the superhero offer.

Jacey headed over to her personal hairdresser, Yuki. She removed the tortoiseshell claw clasp that'd been keeping her hair up. "Do my hair in whatever style you think goes with the jeans vibe. I trust you."

Moments later, Jacey was reclining on a shampoo lounger with her head propped up on the sink while expert hands massaged her scalp, then shampooed and conditioned her hair. Mmmm . . . she *could* have floated away on the sweet sensations—except for the strains of a song she *really* detested: Britney Spears warbled, *"Isn't she lucky, that Hollywood girl? She's so lucky, she's a star, but she cries, cries, cries in the lonely night. . . ."*

Worse was Carlin's shout-out, "This one's for you, Jacey!"

She closed her eyes and willed herself to ignore Carlin and her new musical muse.

"I have a message for you."

Jacey opened one eye. Kia, Cinnamon's stringy-haired assistant, was hovering over her sink and waving a cell phone in her face. Jacey groaned. Obviously, she couldn't catch a break from Cinnamon's nagging. On the screen, Cinn had texted: *One week left.*

The shampoo boy wrapped a thick towel around Jacey's head. Unfortunately, it didn't block her peripheral vision. Carlin strode over, all made-up and looking, frankly, luminous. The uninvited one, thought Jacey, would have jumped at the offer Guy made. Carlin *was* the millions of girls who'd have given anything to be in Jacey's L.A.M.B. sneakers. Would have been, in fact, but for a few hundred votes.

Now, Carlin teased, "If you don't want to take the offer, move over; I'd just die to play Wonder Woman!"

Jacey shocked herself by the words that *almost* came out of her mouth: "Not so fast, sister."

During her hair, makeup, manicure, and pedicure,

Jacey obsessed. Should she forget about the play? About Matt, and everything he'd said to her? Should she just go ahead and say yes, like everyone else thought she should?

"So," said the stylist, Irina, as she led Jacey over to the mirror. "What do you think? A modeling career if the film business doesn't work out?"

Jacey beamed at her reflection. She wasn't vain, and had secretly hated being tagged "the beauty." But, dude, she *had* to give it up for the pros here—they'd done a kick-ass job making her look like model material.

Marcia had done Jacey's ocean-colored eyes in violet liner and volumes of mascara, stained her lips berry, and used just a dab of rosy pink blush on her cheekbones. Yuki had done her hair long and flawlessly tousled, with side-swept bangs. Irina had helped her choose a Tory Burch tone-on-tone flowy silk tank top.

"You guys are the best!" Jacey bowed in a worshipful pose to all of them.

"Ready to model some jeans?" Irina asked with a satisfied grin.

Slickity Jeans came in several styles, from boot cut to flared, reverse-stitch, low-rise, and loose. Each came in either Classic Fit or Skinny.

No way was the slim cut going over Jacey's girly-girl curves. That was probably one of the reasons she'd been chosen for this particular ad—she actually *had* a butt to lift.

"Omigosh! I have the best idea!" Carlin squealed to the assembled team. "Since Jacey can only model the classic fit, how 'bout I wear the skinny cut? Wouldn't that be cool?" She pronounced it *"kewl,"* as if that made it cool. It did not.

Jacey gave a "whatever" shrug and darted into the dressing room. Surprisingly, she actually dug the jeans. They weren't stiff or starchy like most new denim, and the waist didn't pull away in the back. The Slickity Jeans were soft, and conformed easily to her figure. She snuck a look at her butt. Hmmm, maybe it was a little higher.

Over in the next dressing room, she heard Carlin kvetching to Kia, "I'm too narrow for a size zero, even in Skinny! They're gonna have to pin it for me. Times like this, I wish I was plump, like Jacey."

Huh? Jacey checked her tush in the mirror again. Did they make her butt look . . . ? No! She wasn't going down cliché lane.

However, when it came to picking shoes, she went for height—which, as everyone knows, makes you look thinner—sky-high, buttery-soft Christian Louboutin boots did the job just fine.

The art director, Neil, described the pose. Jacey would be standing, holding a pink Razr phone to her left ear, while turning at the waist to peer over her right shoulder. That way, they'd get her full length, from the back and the side. Carlin would sit, leaning forward on a bench several yards back, staring at her enviously. They practiced the setup for a while before breaking for lunch.

It was then that the package arrived. A thick manila envelope, addressed to Jacey. She retreated to the now-deserted makeup area and settled into the chair. Inside was a neatly typed manuscript bound together by three giant butterfly clips. *Fall from Grace*, a three-act play by Rob O'Shay.

The sticky note explained, *Sorry this took so long to get to you. When I told Rob you might consider reading it, he freaked. Man's been slaving over it, up late every night rewriting. It's slammin'!"—Matt*

Jacey took a deep breath, slid out of the designer boots, and read. And read. And kept reading. It was all she could do not to bite her freshly manicured nails, or smudge her makeup with tears. When Jacey was into something, she reacted viscerally. First, her stomach somersaulted. Then it twisted, and finally it plummeted.

She had no idea how much time had passed, because when someone finally called out, "Jacey, we're ready for you. Everyone's in position," she hadn't been Jacey for a while.

She'd been Grace Holloway. Once the most popular girl in her high school, she'd changed her whole life with some tragically bad choices, starting with a cute guy who'd turned ugly after luring her into loving him.

Jacey moved dreamily toward the voices that were calling for her.

"Okay, everyone, we're just about ready. Jacey, we need you back in the boots, standing over there," Neil instructed. Someone handed her the slim cell phone. Someone else poufed out her top so it billowed. Yuki came at her, wielding a curling iron, for a last-minute smooth-out.

Still in a fog, Jacey tried to hold her tears in.

The photographer, peering through the lens, said, "Okay, chin up, Jacey, we'll do a few Polaroids first. Look behind you, happy, happy, happy, lovin' your jeans, lovin' your body!"

There was a lump in her throat.

"Stop," Neil called out. The set director walked over to her. "Jacey, what's wrong?"

She looked up at him. The bright lights nearly blinded her.

"We need you to be with us, honey," he said sweetly. "You seem awfully distracted."

"Sorry." Jacey blinked a few times, but her eyes had already puddled.

"Did you get some bad news?" Yuki was concerned.

"Was it that script you were reading when we were at lunch?" Carlin, who'd missed nothing, now speculated. "Was it a sad story?"

Like the sun peeking out during a rain shower, Jacey smiled through her tears. "No Carlin, it actually turns out to be a very happy story."

The Green Monster

The jealousy monster is in the house! Not just the Malibu beach house, where Jacey treats young Carlin like a slave, but in the photo studio, too. Wanna talk diva? Wanna talk throwing her . . . um . . . weight around during the Slickity Jeans photo shoot? I hear that Jacey insisted Carlin be positioned way in the back, practically out of the ad altogether. I hear she freaked when the jeans barely made it up her hips—especially since Carlin had to have hers pinned. I hear Carlin looked amazing—could Jacey, the beauty, be jealous of the cutie?

Here's a tip, Jace-face: make nice to Carlin, nurture her. She's no threat to you. She's just a sweet, innocent kid from mid-America, looking for a break. You can help her. Do the right thing. The Big Guy would like it.

Chapter Five

Jacey Goes Punk, Cinnamon Goes Berserk

"Oh, my God! Jacey! What have you done to yourself?" Cinnamon shrieked. She slapped her cheeks hard, forcing her mouth into a twisted *O*. Standing in the doorway of Jacey's beach house, the scandalized agent did a pretty fair impression of the painting *The Scream*. Only, not on purpose and not as a joke.

"I've been waiting for the right time to tell you—" Jacey squeaked guiltily. An unannounced visit was not the way she'd envisioned Cinnamon's finding out. "I'm doing this play—"

Cinnamon cringed and covered her face with her hands.

"I just got back from rehearsal—" Jacey started to explain her appearance, but her agent cut in.

"Don't. Say. Another. Word. Unless it's to assure me I'm asleep and having a nightmare. That my star client, just offered the deal of lifetime, did not run a lawn mower up the sides of her head, does *not* have flaming orange spikes masquerading as a hairdo . . . does not have a barbed-wire tattoo around her neck . . . is not covered in black eyeliner . . . shod in steel-tipped motorcycle boots . . . did not get knocked up . . . does not have—please, Lord, no—a pierced eyebrow."

What else could Jacey do but stick her tongue out? The tiny barbell glinted in the sun.

Cinnamon turned white and started to sway dangerously.

"Temporary! Temporary tats," Desi came flying to the door and tucked her shoulder under Cinnamon's arm to hold the terrified agent up.

"It's just just a wig!" Dash was on Desi's heels. He encircled Cinnamon's waist, and the two of them led their wobbly guest inside.

"I couldn't talk her out of a multiple piercing," Ivy sighed. "She'll have holes; we'll have to cover them with makeup." She steered Cinnamon toward an armchair. The agent collapsed into it without any help.

"I think she looks rad!" Carlin-why-she-is-still-here-no-one-knew, chirped. "Show her your black nail polish, Jacey."

"I think Cinnamon's seen enough," Dash said firmly. "How about a latte?"

"Vodka. Straight up," Cinnamon croaked.

"I told you," Ivy wagged a finger at Jacey. "You should have let me tell her about your snap decision to do the play. It's your fault if she has a meltdown,."

"She's a mega power agent," Desi scoffed. "It'll take more than this for a meltdown." She eyed the still-pale Cinnamon. "I think."

"She just needs an explanation," Dash said soothingly. "Um, assurances."

"Do you have assurances to give her, Jacey?" Ivy challenged her cousin.

"I'm going to shower and change," Jacey announced. "I'll explain everything to Cinnamon without the scary visuals."

In her bedroom, Jacey peeled off the torn leather jacket, unhooked the pillow that served as Grace's belly bump, kicked off her motorcycle boots, and replayed the events of the day. Her first rehearsal had been amazing. It had proved that Matt's taste—and her own instincts—were spot-on. *Fall from Grace* was awesome! The play was packed with wonderfully complex characters, and the story was poignant and surprising.

Jacey ripped off the hairpiece, rubbed her scalp, and headed for the shower. She nearly tripped over Carlin's skanky sneakers, which were strewn on the bathroom floor next to a pile of wet towels. Carlin had already overstayed her welcome, and lately Mike was at the beach house a lot, too, with his yappy little dog. The house was becoming *muy* chaotic.

She got into a hot shower and began scrubbing off the temporary tattoos. She smiled, remembering the look on Rob's face when she first strutted into rehearsal. Dressing for the part had been her idea. She'd wanted to surprise him. Mission accomplished! He'd nearly plotzed—a new L.A. word she'd recently learned—when she'd shown up dressed as the Grace Holloway of Act Two.

Up till then, Jacey had known Rob only as a close friend of Matt's—the guy who had helped rescue her from the paparazzi when she'd first arrived in Hollywood. Rob was drop-dead gorgeous, with short, spiky brown hair and killer blue eyes. He was the play-it-cool guy in Matt's posse. Since he didn't have a job, Jacey assumed Matt paid him to be some kind of assistant.

Sure, Rob had mentioned that he was an aspiring playwright. But who wasn't an aspiring *something* in this town? Hollywood was the only place on earth, Jacey thought, as she gave herself a vigorous shampoo, where a plumber was never just a guy with a wrench. Every waiter, salesperson, and club-hopper thought of him or herself as a model, writer, producer, actor, or director. Sometimes they claimed to be all those things at once. Each had come to L.A. awaiting his or her big break.

But Rob had seemed too cute to be taken seriously as a writer. And too hip to seem nervous about anything. This afternoon, the dude formerly known as Mr. Cool had been replaced by Mr. McSweatyou. He'd practically fallen all over himself in his appreciation for her. "I'm so grateful you're doing this, Jacey—it changes everything for me," he'd stammered.

"Just don't forget me when you become a famous playwright," she'd said, looking around for Matt.

Not that she had expected him to be there. He was working, sequestered in a soundproof studio, "looping"—dubbing new dialogue—for his upcoming indie movie, *Dirt Nap*. His commitment to that movie was the reason he couldn't play a role in *Fall from Grace*.

Rob couldn't stop thanking her. "When word got around town that you were interested in *Fall from Grace*, my cell phone nearly blew up. Everyone who rejected me wants to be my agent now! A bunch of backers ponied up the money to produce the play. Jacey, I can actually pay you a little."

"Forget it, I don't need it. Put the money toward your next masterpiece."

"Matt told me you were so generous and real, a sweetheart," Rob had said. "I can see why he said that."

Generous and real? Puke much? That was like saying she was nice. Had a great personality. *What else does he say about me? That he can't get me out of his head? That he wants me?*

Rehearsals and performances were to be held in the aptly named Hole-in-the-Wall Theater. The space was small and spare, and had probably been a community rec room once upon a time. It was way out in an untrendy part of greater Los Angeles.

The rehearsal itself had gone exceptionally well, especially for a first one. The other actors were all newcomers. This was a debut role for many of them. Which didn't mean they weren't good—they kicked butt! Especially the guy playing Duke, the bad boy. Working opposite him, Jacey could see why Grace would fall for him.

That rehearsal made her realize how many talented actors were out there, many of whom would never get a chance to be in a professional production. She felt a twinge of guilt. She really had been so, so lucky.

★ ★ ★

"My bad for not telling you sooner, Cinn," Jacey apologized after showering and getting dressed. She'd removed the barbell from her tongue and brushed her bangs forward to cover the eyebrow ring.

Now that Jacey looked more like her wholesome self again, Cinnamon had relaxed considerably. The vodka probably helped.

"I feel betrayed, Jacey."

Or not.

"It all happened so fast," Jacey rushed to explain. "I only got the script a couple days ago."

Probably not the best thing to say.

"And yet you jumped right in—despite the real offer you got weeks ago." Cinnamon quickly ramped up to exasperated. "You duck my calls, evade my e-mails. I had to ambush you to have a simple conversation—and what happens? I find out you're doing something completely irresponsible. And keeping it secret!"

If ever there were a time for full disclosure, it'd have been now.

"I knew you'd be upset," Jacey admitted. "I was scared to tell you. I'm not great with confrontation, especially with someone I really respect. And to whom I'm so grateful. But I had to do this."

"Had to? Enlighten me." Cinnamon, somewhat mollified by the compliments, leaned forward in her chair.

"It's for my soul." Jacey had no other way to say it.

"Your *what*?" Cinnamon shook her head vehemently. "No, no, and no. It's too soon for your soul. You need to be concerned with your image. Image is everything."

Jacey pictured a capital letter *I*—for "image"—written in the sand. Mentally, she conjured up her own sand-drawn *I*: for "integrity."

"Besides," Cinnamon sniffed, "no one does plays unless they're talking Broadway. You are Jacey Chandliss. You don't even do TV! You're a movie star."

Jacey held her tongue. Otherwise, she'd have asked Cinnamon when it was that she had signed up to be just one thing—but that would have come off as petulant at best, ungrateful at worst.

"You've won this golden opportunity." Cinnamon constantly reminded Jacey of her good fortune. "Now you've been handed another. Why haven't you jumped at this studio offer?"

Jacey sighed. Everything Cinn said was true. She'd seen it with her own eyes that day. The actors in Rob's play were a talented troupe of—in Hollywood parlance—nobodies. None had a "name," a Malibu beach house, or even disposable income. But did fear of the fate of typical

Hollywooders mean she was obliged to jump at every opportunity that came her way? That she was somehow betraying her agent, herself, and unemployed actors the world over if she didn't?

Truth serum: Jacey had still not made a decision about the offer. She'd avoided the subject as long as she could. Thanks to Cinnamon's unfortunate and unannounced house call, *that* train had left the station. She had to come up with something. Now.

"Doing the play, just so you understand, doesn't have anything to do with Mr. Landsman's generous offer—I'm still deciding."

"It has *everything* to do with it!" Cinnamon exploded. "Don't you see? If Guy Landsman finds out about this— this noxious role you're playing—he could take back the offer! Doing a play is bad enough, but this one? A girl who goes homeless, who sleeps around, written by a nobody? It's not your image, and Guy will have a hissy fit if he finds out."

"Is he buying an image—or me?"

"Both."

"*Fall from Grace* has a very limited run; it'll only play for three weeks," Jacey offered. "Then it's over."

"Let me put this plainly, okay, sweetie?" Cinnamon said patronizingly. "If you do this and the offer gets rescinded, it's like taking a winning Powerball lottery ticket and flushing it down the toilet."

Jacey heaved a sigh. Everyone in this town was so dramatic! Translation: if the offer went bye-bye, she'd be letting Cinnamon down. Big time. She'd be letting Ivy, who'd been acting like a Cinna-clone lately, down as well. The only one she wouldn't be letting down was Matt. And Rob, of course.

As if she'd read Jacey's mind, Cinnamon said, "I hope this isn't about Matt Canseco. Not again."

Jacey's cheeks burned.

"How do you think this is going to play with the fans who voted for you, who want to see you wholesome and sweet? What about the Slickity Jeans people? Their entire campaign is resting on you. Not to mention the *Generation Next* producers."

"Is that it?" Jacey retorted. "Who else am I going to let down—the president?"

Cinnamon's cell phone rang. As she listened to the caller, her frustrated face began to soften and take on a healthier glow. The corners of her mouth turned up. If not for the Botox, Jacey was fairly sure she'd have appeared truly animated. Who was on the line? What news could change her mood from *furious*! to *fabulous*! in record time?

"They're talking about you for a Teen Choice Award!" Cinnamon crowed. "Jacey, this is so *fabulous*! So wonderful, such a validation of your talent, all your choices . . . how much your fans love you."

"Really?" Jacey, astonished, sprang up and pumped her fist in the air. "Whoo-hoo! This is so cool!" A hundred questions popped into her head, but all that came out of her mouth was an unabashedly girly squeal.

"What category?" she finally managed.

"Movies—for *Four Sisters*. They're talking you up for Choice Breakout *and* for Choice Hottie."

Impulsively she grabbed Cinnamon and hugged her. Jacey and her friends watched the Teen Choice Awards on TV every year, picking the winners, picking apart what everyone wore, picking the couples most likely to hook up and/or break up. Huge stars like Gwen, Ashton, and Justin won Teen Choice Awards, and *all* of young, hip Hollywood showed up.

Every Jessica—Alba, Biel, Simpson—all the *Pirates of the Caribbean* stars, and all the hot rockers and rappers attended. The ceremony was like the MTV Awards, only not on cable. Translation: cleaner. More wholesome. No wonder Cinnamon was in such a tizzy.

"This makes it even more crucial that you forget about that damned play," Cinnamon declared.

Before Jacey could respond, her friends zoomed into the room.

"What's the whooping about? Something good?" Dash's eyes twinkled.

"Share!" demanded Desi, trailed by surfer-dude Mike and still-in-Malibu Carlin.

"Did you take the superhero offer?" Ivy asked breathlessly. Jacey shook her head no.

Cinnamon went straight to multitasking, doing phone, BlackBerry, and Sidekick all at once, spreading the word and dictating plans to Kia about what she'd instantly dubbed Campaign TCA.

"Do you get to pick which category you want to be in?" Ivy asked no one in particular.

"No, no! Teens vote," answered Desi. "They do it online. If you're one of the top four vote-getters, you're in."

No need to ask how Des, superfan extraordinaire, knew all this. Desi was an awards-show maven.

Jacey put her hand on Cinnamon's arm, blocking her from sending another e-mail. "Wait—you said they're *talking* about me—does that mean I'm nominated in both categories?"

"Not officially," Cinnamon said, keeping her eyes glued to her PDAs. "But talking about you is code for 'you're practically a lock.' We want Choice Breakout, though; it's more prestigious than Hottie. We can nab you that nomination. We do this kind of thing all the time. That's what powerful agents are for. It's a done deal."

"Sweet!" Desi hugged Jacey.

"Baby's first nomination," cooed Dash, stroking her hair. "This calls for a celebration."

The Starlet Shows the Skinny Kid Some Love

Kudos to Jacey. See, it's not all negative. For once, she listened to my excellent advice. Young Carlin had packed her bags and was ready to head back to Cleveland. She was so bummed. She'd gotten a tiny taste of showbiz, but she needed more time to try to make her dream come true. Without money or a job, there was no choice but to go home. That was when Jacey came upon the poor girl, standing in the bathroom, sobbing.

Right then and there, Jacey invited Carlin to spend the entire month at her ritzy Malibu beach house—guess she hasn't forgotten her own roots after all. Or maybe she reads this every day and is starting to atone for those diva moments we all keep hearing about.

Chapter Six

Spending Jacey's Money

He was getting better. Jacey had to give him that much. Him—or her. The he/she-monster who'd become the bane of her existence: the blogger. Previously, the junk that he'd written about her was so outrageous and the lies so bald-faced that she mostly laughed them off. No one she cared about believed any of it. Sure, sometimes her feelings got hurt, but whose wouldn't? The other tabloid darlings didn't seem to let it get to them.

There was something different about these new blog entries. She couldn't pin it down exactly. It was still all bogus. As in, no way had she asked Carlin to stay! The girl was a nuisance and a slob, and was rapidly becoming a parasite. That scene in which Carlin supposedly packed up in tears? Never happened.

Everyone had just assumed she'd go home after the Slickity Jeans shoot.

Carlin hadn't gotten that memo.

The posse had debated. *Ask* her when her flight home was, or *tell* her she had to go? Ivy thought it'd be most effective to throw her stuff out to sea. They were still squabbling about it when the blog entry appeared.

Why the blogger cared about a nobody like Carlin was a mystery to them all. Now Jacey felt she'd been shamed into letting Carlin stay. If she didn't, she risked looking as if she were rescinding her generous offer—which of course she'd never made. Still, she didn't want to come off as a mean cheapskate. Not now, anyway. According to Cinnamon, her image would be tarnished plenty and soon enough.

There was no way Jacey was quitting Rob's play. They'd been rehearsing 24-7 for weeks. Jacey had slipped into her character's skin, and she wore it well. She gave voice to a tattered and torn soul while fulfilling her own. How many actresses got to do that?

Besides, she was convinced Cinnamon was bluffing. The Teen Choice Award–winners were chosen by teens.

Cinnamon might *front* that she could affect the outcome, but Jacey doubted it. Her threat had nothing to do with the play and everything to do with the studio's offer.

When she'd informed Cinnamon of her decision, the agent had appealed to Jacey's friends. "Make her see the light," Cinnamon had begged. "Make her understand that no one wants to see her as some homeless, pregnant punk."

"I would," Dash had responded. "I would go see her in a heartbeat."

"I'm there," echoed Desi. Even Mike the surfer boy chimed in, "Dude, I have no idea what you're talkin' about, but if Des is down with it, ditto."

Even Ivy, conflicted about her loyalty to Jacey versus her feelings about the play, supported Jacey reluctantly.

That was why her friends meant everything to her. Cinnamon ought to know by now that the posse always had her back.

To show her gratitude, Jacey had taken them out and treated them to an all-expenses-paid, too-much-fun, deliberately excessive shopping spree. They'd put a hurtin' on the trendiest streets in town: Robertson and Melrose boulevards. They'd flitted from store to store, loading up on clothes, accessories, and random impulse buys.

All that shopping had made them hungry.

So Jacey called Dolce, a nearby celebrity-friendly hot spot. Prying eyes and paparazzi were discouraged by tall trees that blocked the windows. The food was reputedly excellent and, maybe not so incidentally, Dolce was owned by Ashton Kutcher. Who just might, ya never know, pop in.

While nonceleb guests cooled their heels waiting to be seated, the maitre d' fawned over Jacey and her party and led them straight to a table. A waiter trailed them, schlepping their shopping bags.

Desi's stuff practically needed its own table. Jacey's sweet, petite friend had snared all kinds of adorable merch—dresses, tops, jewelry, makeup. She'd gone superfreak at Victoria's Secret. "Mike," she giggled self-consciously, "likes to see me in pretty underwear."

Turned out Dash had gone fashion glutton this time, too, hitting the men's departments at Gucci, Prada, Tod's, Hilfiger, and Armani. He turned to Jacey abashedly, and said, "Some of this stuff is for Aja. We want to wear it on opening night of the play."

Jacey beamed. "You have great taste, Dash; I'm sure you'll look perfect."

She turned to Ivy, who was usually the most fashion-conscious spendthrift of the group. Ivy had the kind of body that designers designed for—tall and slim but slightly curvy.

Strangely, all Ivy bought was one pair of Sigerson-Morrison gold metallic flats—"for the beach," she explained.

"You can't wear those in the sand," Dash commented. "You'll ruin them."

"Who said anything about walking in them?" Ivy replied. "They're for sand-adjunct, not sand-intense."

"That's it? That's all you got?" Jacey was puzzled. "Come on, admit it, what'd you put on order? What lists did you get on, for what amazing new bag?"

"None."

"Why? What's wrong?" Desi demanded.

"Nothing interested me." Ivy was acting strangely muted.

Jacey squinted, "No? Let's discuss. Dash, What do you think?"

"Shopper's remorse because she's already bought a ton of stuff?" Dash speculated.

"Des?" Jacey asked her opinion.

"Huh?" Des looked up from the menu. "Oh, sorry— What? I was trying to read the menu. Everything's written in a foreign language."

"Perhaps I can help." A spiffily clad waiter materialized. "But first let me welcome Miss Chandliss to Dolce, and offer congratulations on your latest achievement."

Jacey assumed he meant *Galaxy Rangers*, since all

the magazines had reported on the beachfront wrap party. She was about to thank him when he leaned in and stage-whispered, "Of course you know Ashton holds the record for most nominations ever."

Okay, so, not *Galaxy Rangers*.

"But Justin Timberlake has the most wins," Desi piped up. "Even more with 'Sexyback.'" Suddenly, she looked stricken. "Ooops, I didn't just dis Ashton, did I?" She looked around. "Is he here?"

The waiter laughed, assuring her that the star wasn't in. "Now, what part of the menu can I help you with?"

After they had ordered and he was safely out of earshot, Jacey said, "A random waiter knows about the Teen Choice Awards?"

"Hollywood," Desi, Dash, and Ivy all said at once.

"Word spreads faster than E. coli in this town," Dash noted. "The good, the bad, and most especially, the ugly! So just be glad this tidbit about you is in the first category."

"The Breakout Movie category has been won by Orlando Bloom and Jessica Alba," Desi recited. "If you win, you'll be in good company."

"You're just such a fount of info, dearest Des," Dash said.

"The trophy is a surfboard. If you win you'll have to

learn to surf. Mike can teach you!"

"That might be fun." Jacey considered. "Only, it's premature to plan. The surfboard is strictly phantom right now."

The waiter brought their first course—a huge plate piled high with fried calamari, shrimp, and zucchini. Jacey, Ivy, and Dash dug in immediately, stopping only to utter the appropriate *ooohs* and *aaahs* over the rest of Desi's stash: a hobo bag, a Tory Burch printed canvas tote, and a chocolate leather Prada bag.

"From Payless to Prada in under a year," Dash said. "Go, you!"

"Don't forget, from Target to Tracy Reece," Ivy put in.

"You mean that baby-doll dress with the ruffles? How cute did that look on me? I had to have it. Didn't I?" Desi turned to Jacey. "It's returnable, if you think I went overboard."

"Don't be ridiculous, Des," Jacey said, as the busboy cleared the table to make room for their entrees. "You crave, I cave. It's the least I can do."

"Speaking of returnable," Ivy sniffed, "can we just pause to reflect on What. Carlin. Bought. And, how much longer before we get to return her?"

The uninvited one had managed get invited to their shop-op, snagging pricey Armani frameless sunglasses and a traffic-stopping Heatherette bikini. "It's just like the one Pamela Anderson wore on a yacht one time," Carlin had burbled joyfully. "It's a fashion statement—ship-wrecked socialite."

"And don't let's forget the full cache of La Perla bras and panties," Ivy said.

"Makes you wonder who she's planning on impressing," Jacey giggled.

"Whoever he is, I hope he doesn't turn up in my room," Desi said.

"I hope he does," Ivy said. "That would be reason enough to kick her bony butt out."

Their main dishes arrived. Jacey bit off a corner of her pumpkin ravioli to see if she actually liked it.

"Well, at least she didn't insist on tagging along for lunch," Dash said.

Carlin had cited "elsewhere to be."

"Where would *elsewhere* be?" Ivy asked.

"Date with Kia," Desi responded.

"Our Kia?" Jacey's eyebrows shot up. "Cinnamon's assistant?"

"The drippy one herself," Ivy replied.

"I can't see those two as friends at all. What do they have in common?" Jacey asked.

Three pairs of eyes stared at her. "You!"

Jacey shrugged. That was a pretty superficial bond. But whatevs.

"There you are, our newly minted nominee!" A male voice broke into their convo, followed quickly by a pat on Jacey's back.

"Adam," Jacey turned to look up at him. "I know *you* know I don't have the nomination yet." She tried to squash her annoyance at her erstwhile costar and all-star hanger-on. He often happened to turn up wherever she was.

"With *your* agent? Are you kidding? It's in the bag," he said confidently.

"C'mon, Adam, the teens vote for it—" Desi said.

"Oh, sweet naïveté. Sure they do, sure they do."

"You know something, don't you, Adam?" Dash intuited. "Or at least you think you do."

Adam took that as a cue to join them. He lugged a heavy leather chair over and made himself comfortable. "I have news."

"Spill," Dash demanded.

Adam made a big show of checking out the restaurant to make sure nobody "important" could overhear them. Then he stage-whispered loud enough that anyone could have: "Jacey and I are invited to be presenters at the Teen Choice Awards. She's *so* nominated."

"Where'd you come by this bit of info?" Dash asked.

"And how come we don't know about it?" Ivy asked, miffed.

Adam raised his palms. "I come to you in total truthiness. Don't take my word for it, call Cinnamon. Your indefatigable agent will tell you."

Dash went for his cell phone, but Ivy stopped him. "I'll call Cinn; I've gotta make a pit stop in the ladies' room anyway." With that, she excused herself.

Meanwhile, Adam had insinuated himself completely into their lunch.

"So, what do you think?" He jabbed Jacey's arm playfully. "This year, you and me, presenters? Next year, you and me, double nominees?"

"Really? In what categories?" Jacey indulged him.

"Are you kidding?" Adam feigned surprise. "*Galaxy Rangers*? Choice Chemistry is ours. But I bet we also get it for Lip Lock." He winked.

"In your dreams, Pratt," Jacey said, wincing.

"So we should probably just go together," added Adam, picking up a fork and spearing one of her uneaten ravioli.

"We should?" Jacey asked.

"It's not like you have a boyfriend. I don't see a lot of . . . candi-*dates*," he riffed. "Everyone's gonna see us onstage together anyway. I'll be your date."

"Whoa, down, boy," Jacey chastised him. "Why do you assume I don't have a date?"

He gave her a look. "What? Like Matt Canseco's gonna step up? Get real, Chandliss."

Her cheeks burned.

"Yeah, I saw the tabloids, too: you and Canseco on the beach during the wrap party," Adam rambled. "The difference is, I'm *from* this town. I know a doctored photo when I see one. Those pictures don't even look like you two!"

Desi laughed so hard some of her drink came out her nostrils.

Dash grabbed his gut, doubled over with laughter.

Adam was so genuinely clueless that Jacey couldn't mock him. Twisted as it sounded, there was something genuine in his bluster. She almost felt sorry for him.

Almost. But not quite.

Adam left, finally understanding that he'd goofed. Those pictures of Jacey and Matt were real. Still, Jacey promised to "think about" her Teen Choice date. It was only when the waiters arrived to clear the table that Jacey realized Ivy had never returned from the ladies' room.

"I'm-a check on her, see if she fell in," Jacey decided. "Go ahead and order dessert for us."

Ivy was not all right.

Chapter Seven

Ivy's Confession

Jacey's cousin was not in the Ladies'. Nor had she returned to their table.

After searching the block, Jacey found Ivy outside, all the way around the corner from the restaurant. She was sitting by the side of the curb and appeared to be on the phone.

"Jacey!" Ivy seemed alarmed. "I was just about to come back in." She quickly folded the phone and fumbled for her dark glasses. She got them on, but not before Jacey saw that her eyes were red and puffy. She clutched a tissue in her fist.

"What did Cinnamon say?" Jacey was worried now. If Ivy was that upset, it must be bad, something her cousin was afraid to tell her. "What? Did I not get the nomination? It's not worth crying about, Ivy. As Matt says, you stay winsome, you lose some." She flashed Ivy a supportive smile.

"Why do you assume this is about you?" Ivy asked indignantly.

"I . . . I . . . It's just . . ." Jacey stammered, surprised and stung.

"It isn't always, you know," Ivy said softly.

Jacey sat down and draped her arm around her cousin. "My bad. That was selfish. Can we do over?"

Ivy slipped out of Jacey's embrace. "I did get in touch with Cinnamon—and Pratt had it right. You've been invited to present Choice Reality Show at the awards. Naturally, Cinnamon refused to sign off until they confirmed your nomination."

"O-*kay*," Jacey said slowly, "but what's going on with *you*? Why having you been acting so weird—you hardly even bought anything today."

Ivy ignored the question. "By the way, Cinnamon got you an extension from Landsman, since you already passed the deadline. You have more time to make the decision."

"You're not making this easy, Ives. I really do want to know what's bumming you out."

"And when I'm ready to tell you, I will," Ivy said, her

voice breaking. "I didn't ask you to come find me."

"Is it Emilio?"

"No. It's nothing. Forget it," Ivy sniffed.

Chastised, Jacey raised her hands in mock surrender. "I'm not saying anything right, am I?"

"It doesn't matter." Ivy stood up and started back toward the restaurant. They walked in silence. Jacey was ticked at herself for not sensing that something was off with Ivy earlier and totally lost about why. Had she done something to cause it? She racked her brain.

"I never really thanked you," Jacey said gently, "for taking my side about the play when Cinnamon threatened me with Teen Choice excommunication. Especially since I know you were against it."

"I'm not thrilled," Ivy conceded. "I hate the whole situation. But you know I have your back, no matter what. She added, "Cinnamon is totally scrambling to keep the offer alive now that Landsman found out about the play. "

Of course Landsman had found out. Jacey still didn't believe he'd rescind the offer because of a small, limited-run production in an out-of-the-way theater. "What did Cinn say when the Big Guy confronted her?"

"She told him she's talking you out of it."

Jacey laughed. Classic Cinnamon. "Why am I not

surprised? So what'll happen when it opens, and I'm obviously in it?"

"She's working her tail off for you, against her own better judgment." Ivy's tone turned fierce. "Stalling Landsman, protecting you, working to make sure you get the nomination. You're lucky to have her."

Why was Ivy suddenly Cinnamon's BFF?

As they circled back to Dolce, Ivy slowed her pace. Jacey could see that Ivy was struggling to decide whether or not to tell her what she was thinking.

Jacey's phone rang. "Hi, Dash . . . yeah, I'm with her. . . . No, you guys take the car, go home. We'll be back soon."

That seemed to be Ivy's cue. "This is really hard." She began to open up. "I . . . I . . . don't know how to say this, how to ask you—"

Out of the corner of her eye, Jacey noticed that a small clutch of tweens had gathered near some boutiques on Melrose. They were pointing at her, whispering excitedly, working up the courage to approach her.

"Just say it!" Jacey demanded impatiently.

So, it was right in the middle of the most trafficked, noisy stretch of bustling Melrose Avenue—motors running, horns honking, shoppers chatting—in front of a bunch of giddy fans, thrilled with their luck at bumping into a star, that Ivy blurted out, "I want you to take Landsman's offer. Now."

"What?" Jacey was shocked. This wasn't even close to anything she might have imagined Ivy was going to say. In a daze, she signed autographs and posed for a couple of pictures before begging off, taking Ivy by the elbow and scooting back inside the safety of the restaurant. Jacey signaled to the maitre d' that she didn't want to be disturbed.

"That's what you're crying about? I don't get it. I mean, why do you care that much?" Jacey was stumped.

Ivy had an answer ready. "Isn't this why we're here? This takes you to the next level. There's no downside. 'Cause if *Galaxy Rangers* flops, then what? If you didn't take the offer, you might as well say good-bye to the career that's gotten off to such an amazing jump start. You could be a has-been just like that. And I know you, Jacey, it'd kill you." Ivy had removed her sunglasses and pinned Jacey with a red-eyed stare.

"There's got to be something else," Jacey deduced, "or you wouldn't be this upset."

Was it the money? They'd all been bitten by the spending bug, but when had Ivy become so bling-obsessed that the idea of Jacey turning down such a rich payday freaked her out?

"I will get other roles; we still have lots of money. . . ." Jacey trailed off. ". . . I think."

"It's not that." Ivy paused. "Okay, I admit I've found a friend in spending. But I wouldn't ask you just for that."

"Then what?"

Ivy cleared her throat, twisting the tissue around in her fingers. "You were the star of our family before *Generation Next*, before you came to Hollywood and made it big. You were always the center of attention, putting on your little plays for us, doing those modeling gigs. We all came to see you in the local theater and in school plays. It was always Jacey this and Jacey that. We stood by you, supported you. We were your first and most enthusiastic audience—we still are."

Jacey swallowed and lowered her eyes. She could practically see the word *guilty* etched on the table.

"I was the cousin, the smart girl," Ivy continued, "I took the risk-free, expected-of-me, straight-and-narrow route. Don't misunderstand; I was always proud of you. I was never jealous of your talent, or your looks, or even all the attention. The only thing I envied was that you always knew what you were going to do."

"I didn't—" Jacey started to protest she'd never expected to end up in Hollywood so soon, but Ivy stopped her. "You were born to be an actress. It was only a matter of time before you got here."

"Isn't there something you wanted to do?" Jacey squeaked meekly, realizing—oops!—that she'd never thought about Ivy's goals.

"I never had passion for anything, not like you—until now."

"Now?" Jacey gulped.

"Yeah, Jace, I do. It's thanks to you, of course! For inviting me out here. This is a world I never would have dreamed of. Not for me, anyway. But now that I've seen how this works—show business—I can not only see myself in it, I can see myself being passionate, gifted—and truly happy. It turns out that you're not the only girl who came here from Michigan and got to live her dream."

"Go on," Jacey said, as it slowly dawned on her that Ivy had given this a lot of thought.

"I think I could be . . ." Ivy stumbled a moment. "Like Cinnamon. An agent. Work my way up from assistant to junior agent. God knows, creepy Kia can barely keep up— Cinnamon's wasting her time with her. But me . . ."

"You guys have talked about it?" Jacey was surprised. Something else she hadn't noticed.

"A little."

"That's . . . that's . . . terrific. You want to be an

agent—I'm totally for that. I'm a hundred percent behind you." Jacey scrunched her forehead, still trying to connect the dots. "Call me lame, but I don't understand how my taking Landsman's offer has anything to do with it."

In the pained silence that followed, Jacey got her answer. Hello! Ivy wanted Cinnamon to hire her, to train her. Cinnamon wanted Jacey to take the offer. If it looked as if Ivy had persuaded her, Ivy would look good to Cinnamon. She'd be a lock, on her way to making her dream a reality.

"Is that why you're so against me doing the play? Because when Landsman finds out Cinnamon didn't talk me out of it, he might kill the offer? And you think that would kill your chances with Cinnamon?" The words tumbled out before Jacey could censor herself, let alone hide her feelings, which were caught at the intersection of wildly annoyed and mildly betrayed.

"I knew I shouldn't have asked you. Emilio said you'd think that." There was a catch in Ivy's voice.

So Ivy had discussed this with Emilio, too. Which pissed Jacey off even more and led her to sputter, hurtfully, "Did you already make a deal with Cinnamon? You deliver me— she hires you?"

Ivy's jaw dropped. "You can't think that."

Jacey never would have. Not a year ago. But Ivy had

changed. It was clear that her cousin had been the one most easily seduced by Hollywood. Ivy demanded like a diva, spent like a millionaire, behaved like an entitled elitist, and clearly had her sights set on bigger, better, more.

"What should I think, Ivy?"

"I'm going to be brutally honest, Jacey." Her expression was dead serious, and it scared Jacey a little. "I am asking you to do something for me—absolutely, that's true. *But*, also, something I believe is truly in your best interest. And . . ."—she paused, going in for the kill—"I think your unrequited crush on Matt is blinding you. And that maybe it's time to listen to someone who really cares about you. And theoretically, someone you care about."

"That's not fair, Ivy!" Jacey protested. "You just sprung this on me. You never said you wanted to become an agent."

"Maybe you were never listening. Or observing. I'm telling you now. Have you become such a big star that you can't see anything clearly?" Ivy countered. "When did you become that tunnel-visioned—and that selfish?"

"When did you become that underhanded, making deals with my agent behind my back?" Jacey shot back.

Ivy's eyes clouded up. She rooted around in her bag for another tissue and blew her nose. "I didn't make any deals with anyone. I would never do that to you. And if you don't believe me . . . well, maybe . . . maybe . . . we need to rethink our relationship. You can't choose your relatives, but maybe we have no business being friends."

Jacey bit her lip. No, she wasn't going to cry.

"I'm sorry if what I'm about to say hurts you, Jacey, but here it is: I'm not just a cipher. I have my own opinions. I was, and still am, against you doing the play, but not for the reason you think. It's not about your image, or my friendship with Cinnamon, or my own goals. I don't like to see you being used—and Matt is using you. Think about it. Now that he got what he wanted—you starring in Rob's play—has he even called you? Seen you? Texted you?" Ivy challenged. "You don't even know what he's doing—or . . ." she trailed off.

"Or who—who he's doing it with? Isn't that what you want to say?" Jacey fought to choke down the hard knot in her throat—and lost. Tears streamed down her face. Ivy had the final word. "Doing the play won't make Matt love you, Jacey."

The last dress rehearsal for *Fall from Grace* took place the night after Jacey and Ivy's unpretty confrontation. Jacey was never more relieved to get into her character's skin. The vibe at the beach house was tense. The cousins barely spoke. Dash and Desi were caught awkwardly between them, and clueless Carlin didn't know anything was wrong.

Jacey was glad to get away from all that. Still, the dress rehearsal marked her worst performance ever.

"I'm sorry," she apologized to Rob and her cast members after they'd finished. "That sucked. I'm off my game today."

Rob massaged her shoulders and said soothingly, "Last-minute jitters. It just means you'll be that much better tomorrow."

"Opening night" was what he meant. A sour taste came up in her throat. Suddenly she dreaded the next day. And not because of stage fright. It was because of the jarring realization that her personal drama was affecting her stage drama. That was unprofessional, way worse than opening-night jitters. How could Ivy choose *now* to stress her out so much?

What were the chances, she thought, drifting over to the watercooler, that she could make up with Ivy before the following night? Ivy had accused her of being selfish. *So* not true! Jacey had included her friends in everything; they all benefited from her generosity. Desi sent money home to help her family, and Dash had been able to enroll in college.

Ivy had called that superficial.

What a joke, since she was the one who'd obviously loved the luxe life most!

Jacey brought the paper cup to her lips and chewed nervously on the curled edge. Unless she caved, it was doubtful they'd make up—not by tomorrow. Or ever, she thought with a sinking feeling.

"So, Dimples, is that really you? Sweet, wholesome Jacey, covered with tattoos, pierced tongue, dyed spikes?" The deep male voice hit her like a kick in the gut and turned her legs to jelly. Her water cup slipped to the floor.

"Matt," she stammered. *Nice of you to show up*, was what she almost said. Chilly was how she almost acted. But his hair was all brushy bed-head, his eyes were all heavy-lidded, and his lips were sweetly curved and slightly parted. She melted.

"So, I hear the outfit and the makeup was all your idea—your interpretation of Grace. That took guts. No one would recognize the real you," Matt said admiringly.

"Sometimes I wonder who the real *you* is, Matt," Jacey said, channeling Ivy.

"Whoa, what's that supposed to mean—or are you still in character?"

"Are *you*?"

"Jacey, c'mon, give me a clue. You mad at me? What'd I do?"

Maybe it *was* her nerves about the next day. Or the need to blame someone for today's crap rehearsal. Could have been her confusion, his continual mixed messages. But most likely it was Ivy. 'Cause no matter how Jacey dissected it, what Ivy had said could still be true.

In a strangled voice she said, "I need to know the truth about something, Matt. Did you use the way I feel about you to convince me to do this, so Rob could get his play showcased?"

"Is that what you think?" If he wasn't astonished and hurt, he was a damned good actor.

She didn't answer.

He turned the tables on her. "Here's *my* question. Are you affected by this part? Does the character speak to you? Has she gotten under your skin? Compared with, say, your part in *Galaxy Rangers*?"

"Rhetorical questions." She was miffed. "You know the answers. And you haven't answered mine."

"You're overthinking, Jacey. Maybe you're nervous about tomorrow."

"Don't patronize me, Matt, please." Now she was

getting angry, especially because he was right on about her being nervous.

"Here's the bottom line. I read this play. I pictured you in it. End of story."

"Except for the part where you made sure to tell me about it, to pique my interest."

"You're conveniently forgetting the circumstances," Matt said gently.

"Believe me, Matt, I remember every detail of the day you happened to mention it," she said, tearing up.

"So, do you remember being so freaked out you bolted into the ocean? Do you remember not caring about the big movie-star offer—and feeling guilty? Do you remember asking me for advice?"

She hung her head, embarrassed.

"Talented artists need to flex different muscles, try new things," Matt said seriously. "Otherwise, you run the risk of repeating yourself and never growing. So when you freaked out at the wrap party, it all came together. *Fall from Grace* was a way for you to get that, firsthand. Plus, it was something you could do quickly, before you got tied up in another movie. I thought I'd be helping. If there was an agenda, it was to remind you how talented you really are, Jacey."

Her righteous anger had evaporated. But not her doubts.

"And, *yeah*," he continued, "if it helps another friend, like Rob, in the process, I'm sorry, I don't see a downside."

If it helps a friend. It wasn't Rob she was picturing. It was Ivy.

"And anyway," Matt broke into her thoughts, "I didn't force you to take the role. All I did was send you the script."

Liar! she wanted to scream. *You stroked my arm and my hair, you said I was cute, with a perfect butt. Or something. You were about to kiss me.*

"Does that justify you toying with my emotions?" Jacey crossed her arms defensively.

"How'd I do that?"

"Oh, Matt." She sighed. "You know how I feel—felt—about you. I told you. I showed you. You rejected me. And then, that night in the cove . . ."

Softly, he interjected, "I didn't reject you Jacey. I'm sorry if you took it that way. I was honest. I said I was attracted to you—who wouldn't be? I told you I could never be 'that guy' for you. Exclusivity—that's what you'd want. It's not my thing. I'd only hurt you if I made promises I couldn't keep."

"Spare me the martyr speech," she mumbled, though

the fight was out of her. "It's just, you got all romantic on the beach, coincidentally telling about this play your friend wrote. It smells like you were playing me, just to get me to do *Grace.*"

Matt shook his head and started to walk away. "If you think that, you don't know me. And if you were hurt—I'm sorry, but it proves my point. 'Cause that was no act. I wasn't playing you. That was me, in the moment. A beautiful sunset on the beach in Malibu, a beautiful girl next to me. . . It was impulsive. It was a mistake. That's who I am, Dimples."

Jacey's Hot Mess of the Week!

Not good times for our starlet. Her cousin is steam-ing mad at her; her agent—Cinnamon Jones—is furious, and thinking about dropping her; and, for the bonus round, Matt Canseco has broken up with her! Whoa, all this just before opening night of her ill-conceived play. It's a good thing she still has Carlin in her corner.

Chapter Eight

Opening Night

"You're wrong, Mother," she said softly. "I never had it all. Just the pressure to be it all. There are things that happened I won't ever tell you. Things that can't be changed. But I can change. And I did. I realized that there's only one thing I want, and it isn't status, or money, or popularity. It's feeling needed. And where I am now, in this shelter, helping those who need it most—I'm truly needed. I'm the lucky one. I'm not Grace-the-fallen, I'm Grace, truly blessed."

At Jacey's last line, the stage lights dimmed.

The applause didn't come right away. Too many people were still sobbing. When the response to *Fall from Grace* finally did begin, it built, from loud and enthusiastic to eardrum-shattering.

Oh, my God, thought Jacey, as she reached out to grasp the hands of her fellow actors. *We did it. We freakin' did it.*

The crowd, a couple of hundred or so—as many as the Hole-in-the-Wall Theater could squeeze in—were now on their feet. They were clapping wildly, whistling shrilly through two fingers, and expressing their appreciation for a performance that'd blown them away.

What flashed through Jacey's mind? *This is the best night of my life!* She was flushed, beaming from head to toe, tingling all over. Had she ever known such pure bliss? She'd shed her character now. These feelings were all hers; they belonged to Jacey Chandliss, actress.

She'd been brilliant. They'd all—she shot a megawatt smile at the rest of the cast—been brilliant. They'd made the improbably poignant story of Grace Holloway come alive for these cheering, tearful people.

Impulsively, Jacey took a step forward and signaled the audience to hold its applause. She took a deep breath and called out for Rob O'Shay to come up onstage.

Rob, too nervous to sit during the performance, had been pacing the aisles the whole time. Now, he ran up and on to the stage and hugged Jacey so hard that he nearly knocked the wind out of her. When he let go, she saw tears clouding his indigo blue eyes. He couldn't speak.

So, Jacey did. "I just wanted to be sure everyone knows that Rob wrote *Fall from Grace*. It's his first play! How amazing it that? I predict that after tonight, he'll be on everyone's buzz list, the new 'It' playwright!"

The first few rows of the theater exploded with applause. They consisted of Rob's family, his on-again actress girlfriend, Gina Valentine, and his closest friends, Emilio, Aja, and Matt.

Jacey's posse was also up front. Even Ivy had tabled their quarrel for the night. Aside from friends and kin of the rest of the cast, the audience was composed of actors, up-and-coming playwrights, producers, directors, and a smattering of VIPs. Some had come for the drama, others to satisfy their curiosity. And some—reporters and reviewers—were working.

"Jacey! Down here, it's me!"

Desi was just below her at the lip of the stage, cradling a huge bouquet of roses. From Matt?

Desi shouted above the applause, "From your parents."

Jacey teared up again. Family, the people who supported you always. Like Ivy.

Jacey had expected the opening-night party to be at a club like Mood, or Koi, or Hyde Lounge—any of the glitzy, celebri-studded nightspots sure to attract media attention. But Rob had surprised them all, opting for sentiment over sizzle.

The *Fall from Grace* afterparty was held at Dungeon, the underground dive bar in a sketchy neighborhood so out of the way even the paparazzi didn't follow people there. Dungeon was the place where Matt's friends had first met Jacey's four months earlier. That night had truly gotten their West Coast adventure off to a kickin' start.

Dungeon hadn't dressed for an opening-night celebration. Dank and dingy as ever, the space was permanently infused with a heady aroma of marijuana mixed with beer. A contact high was assured the minute one walked through the door! There was no waitstaff, only the orange-skunk-streaked bartender, Tina, who welcomed them with open arms, kegs of beer, and fare that ranged from greasy (nachos) to greasier (cheese-topped potato skins) to fried (calamari), more fried (wings), and deep-fried (mozzarella sticks).

It could not have been more perfect. "Ah," Dash joked, "the roar of the crowd, the smell of the grease-fries."

By the time Jacey arrived (after scrubbing all traces of the character she'd played from her body, then posing for a few pictures outside the theater), the party was in full swing. The VIP guests swarmed her like bees startled out of their nest, buzzing, gushing, raving, and heaping piles of praise on her "sterling," "brilliant," "genius," "bravura" performance.

Some people even seemed sincere.

"You rocked!" A joyful Desi, trailed by her surfer boy, Mike, greeted her excitedly. Mike belched, then repeated his earlier rave review.

Emilio, muscular, tan, and grinning hugely, pumped her hand. "You killed, Jacey. This is gonna make Rob's career." Ivy, nearly a head taller than her boyfriend, hovered behind him. She leaned in to give Jacey a peck on the cheek. "Congratulations, cousin," she murmured.

Then Dash and Aja were there, and she fell gratefully into a tight, three-way hug. Dash whispered in her ear, "Amazing Jace—that's what we're gonna call you from now on. You never stop surprising me—and reminding me why we're really here."

Jacey muffled a sob. Dash got her. Dash loved her. Dash would never desert her, never pressure her into making a decision. She squeezed his arm. *Stay with me, please*, she signaled.

For every person who'd really wanted to see the show, there were two who'd come hoping to see Jacey fall on her face. Hollywood was probably the only place on earth where someone else's failure was perceived as a personal victory.

Learning to recognize the jealous insults when they blended so effortlessly with congrats was a skill. At other times the insults, disguised as backhanded compliments, were as thinly veiled as a naked body under a see-through teddy.

It helped to be surrounded by friends. Jacey felt less vulnerable.

"Incoming," Dash whispered in her ear.

"That was so brave!" Sierra Tucson, wearing a short metallic dress, cooed effusively. "Doing a play could kill your career—you're such the risk-taker."

"Here's to ya." Kate Summers, Sierra's sister in spite, was already sloshed. She raised a stein of beer unsteadily. "What a waste to dress up—where's the paparazzi when you need them?" With that, the Gucci-clad actress drained her glass.

What was up with her? Clueless was Kate's natural state; tonight she was nonsensical *and* borderline hostile.

Jacey was almost glad to see Carlin and Kia insert themselves into the group, until Carlin opened her mouth.

"I don't know how you did it!" The slinky one was all blond Barbie bangs and sugary princess voice. "You're so different in real life than that Grace."

"That's why they call it acting," Desi cracked.

"Well, I *know* that!" Carlin waved her away dismissively. "But Jacey's just so sweet and nice and gentle. She'd never get mixed up with a wild guy."

You'd be surprised, Jacey couldn't help thinking.

"Can you give me some tips?" Carlin asked. "On playing against type?"

"It's all on the page," Jacey quipped, knowing she'd stumped her unwanted houseguest.

The blank look confirmed it. None of them, not Carlin, Kate, Sierra—or even Kia, who *should* have known—had ever heard the famous showbiz saying *If it's not on the page, it's not on the stage.* Meaning: if the writer hasn't created the character in the first place, the actor can't bring her to life.

"Rob wrote the story. If not for that, there'd be no play," Dash interpreted.

"But it took the right actress to make it accessible," Dash's boyfriend, Aja, added, "to make the audience really believe her."

"Was there anything about the character you could relate to?" Kia, drab in her usual black, suddenly asked Jacey. It was almost weird to hear her speak up.

Carlin responded. "In the beginning, when Grace is so

popular, and everyone loves her, wants to be her—that's like Jacey's life in high school, right? I read about it so many times."

"Trust me, not everyone wanted to be me," Jacey protested. "I didn't run the cool clique like Grace does. I was a drama nerd."

"Don't be modest, Jace." Ivy had appeared, grasping an uncorked bottle of wine. "You *were* a big deal in school. You had a million friends and dated the hottest guy. I should know, I was there."

Jacey cringed. Was Ivy going to keep reminding her of how great she had it, over and over again?

"The hottest guy dumped me on prom night," Jacey said faux-sweetly. "Surely you remember, Ives. Like you said, you were there."

"But Grace was envied, and—" Kia started.

"Beautiful," Carlin finished the sentence. "Just like you, *Generation Next*'s beauty."

"And yet"—Jacey was desperate to get off that subject—"I hardly had a miserable home life. I wasn't abused. I never felt the kind of pressure Grace does to be perfect. I feel more pressure out here than I ever did at home." Now she looked daggers at Ivy.

"Jacey's parents are very cool," Dash added. "No secrets in the closet chez Chandliss Taylor."

"But"—Carlin pointed a manicured finger at Jacey—"you do have a stepdad, so who knows, maybe your real dad is out there somewhere and he did something bad."

Jacey's jaw dropped. How could Carlin say something like that?

"Snap!" Carlin threw her head back, guffawing. "Gotcha! I was just kidding, right, Kia?"

Kia, who'd been immersed in her BlackBerry, looked up nervously. "Texting Cinnamon," she explained.

Jacey felt a stab of sadness. Had Cinnamon been there, the night would have been perfect. But her agent had given her a heads-up that she would not, could not come to the play, and Jacey understood.

"So what's Cinnamon saying? Is she ballistic?" Jacey pressed Kia.

"Obviously, Guy Landsman knows she didn't talk you out of the play," Dash said. "How's she handling that?"

"Uh, wait—don't know yet." Kia fumbled with her PDA.

Kia was lying. The sudden realization stunned Jacey. But why? Of course Cinnamon knew. No doubt her agent had already left a dozen messages on her cell phone and Sidekick. So who was the girl really texting?

"Anyway," Carlin babbled on, "you sure didn't end up like Grace, going off with some scary motorcycle guy who ripped her off, knocked her up, and left her."

Jacey finally extracted herself and made her way to the buffet, where she dived hungrily into buffalo wings, mozzarella sticks, and nachos as she greeted more well-wishers. "Where's Rob?" She asked Desi.

Desi hitched her thumb toward the bar. "Polluted, according to Emilio."

Jacey was about to get up and head over there when Rob caught her eye and stumbled toward her. He was, as the saying goes, feeling no pain.

"Jacey! Did I tell you how good you did?" Rob slurred. "You made everyone love her, love you, love me, love the whole world!" He spread his arms out to take in all of Dungeon, then promptly lost his balance.

Aja and Dash reached out and propped him up.

The party had been going strong for hours by the time Matt swung by. Jacey was dancing with Dash, Aja, and Adam when she spotted him. Where had he been since the play? Jacey wondered. Wearing creased brown denim jeans and a faded, cocoa-colored work shirt that accentuated his dark hair and liquid eyes, he looked . . . good enough to eat. She signaled to him to come join her on the dance floor.

He raised his beer bottle, toasting her, but didn't come over until he had made the rounds of his peeps. Later, he squeezed her arm, pecked her cheek, and whispered, "You did good, Dimples." Then he walked away.

What had she been expecting? That he'd embrace her, kiss her passionately, spirit her away to some private place? After she'd accused him of using her?

Jacey watched Matt make his way to the bar and get into a deep convo with a group that included Rob's girlfriend, an overly touchy-feely-flirty (probably hammered) Carlin, and her shadow, Kia.

Didn't matter. Jacey refused to allow Matt's aloofness to ruin her night. No matter what Matt's motives had really been, didn't it all work out for the best?

Well, that depended who you asked.

Over the next several days, Jacey heard it all. Landsman, predictably, went crazy, acting more like a spurned lover than a major studio honcho. "I was going to make her the biggest star this town has ever seen; then she goes and performs this . . . this filth!" he'd ranted.

It didn't matter that *Fall from Grace* was getting rave reviews from *everyone*. In Guy's opinion, the star of their hoped-for family-event franchise had gone to the dark side. He turned his fury on Cinnamon, whom he actually tried to fire, forgetting that she didn't work for him. He tried to intimidate, using the creaky old cliché "She'll never eat lunch in this town again." Meaning: he had the power to hurt Jacey's career and wasn't above using it.

Cinnamon was surprisingly serene about everything, pointing out that even though Landsman was mad, he'd never actually said he no longer wanted Jacey for his movies.

"He's waiting for the *L.A. Times* review," Ivy told Jacey. Their Arts section had not yet weighed in. That was what counted in Guy's world. The following Sunday, he went silent. The review was simple and to the point: *Until further notice, Jacey Chandliss is Hollywood's best young actress.*

Jacey Dumps Fans!?!

Jacey shuns fans! Hogs spotlight! It wasn't bad enough that she took on a despicable role that shocked her fans, but now that the first reviews are raves, Jacey is claiming the spotlight, saying that *she* made the play a success. Which isn't sitting well with her costars. As for the few faithful fans who trekked to that out-of-the-way shack to see her? Jacey brushed right past them, without bothering to sign one measly autograph, let alone show the gratitude she should be showering on them. At the afterparty, Jacey's spotlight-hogging ways continued. She arrived late and left early, fighting with her cousin, Ivy, and spurned by her ex, Matt Canseco.

Payback's a bitch, Jacey, and I predict you'll be getting yours real soon. Karma's gonna catch up with you. You're headed for heartbreak city.

Chapter Nine

Nomination Nation

Jacey sank into the sun-kissed sand, giving herself over to complete and total relaxation. It was Monday, her one day off from performing in *Grace*. Intent on luxuriating in every last second, she'd come out early and planted herself on a towel by the ocean, mere yards from her front porch.

The tiny, sparkling grains of sand beneath her were soft and pliable, instantly forming to her contours.

She cast her gaze out to sea, where whitecaps glistened like crystals on a glass ocean. She listened to the sounds of the lapping waves as they gave the shore a lick, then pulled back. Kind of like Matt, she reflected: giving her a taste of him, then pulling back. She breathed in the salt air, felt the gentle sunlight playing upon her face, the softest breeze caressing her body. Who knew a girl from a subdivision in Michigan could feel so whole here? And lovin' acting in a tiny indie play seen by a paltry few hundred people a night?

Incredibly, Jacey found more layers in Grace with each performance. The audience members, in turn, found new ways to show their appreciation. Bouquets of flowers were routinely tossed onto the stage; some guy even flung his Jockeys at her on the third night.

She was flattered and grateful, but an adoring audience wasn't the only reason she came home feeling great every night. Jacey could no longer deny the *truthiness*—as Adam Pratt, channeling Stephen Colbert, would say—of the situation. The play nourished her, just like the sand, the sea, and sun were doing right now. Matt called this kind of acting flexing the muscles. Jacey called it feeding her soul.

She really did have it all. Meaningful work, pampered ease in the Malibu sun; what more could anyone want? She'd already asked her business manager to extend the lease on the Malibu pad. No one in her posse complained about that!

The only glitch was that Ivy was still mad at her. And Carlin, president of "Guests Without Borders," just stayed.

And flirted with anyone in pants, including Mike, which drew Desi's wrath.

They could, Jacey mused, curling her toes in the sand, stay in Malibu indefinitely. Ditch the house she'd felt pressured into buying in Beverly Hills. Get something even bigger, right there on the beach. If she accepted Landsman's offer, she could have her own Malibu McMansion. Permanently. Then her family could come whenever they wanted—all their families could. She'd have her whole world, all the people she cared about, with her whenever she wanted. How exceedingly cool would that be?

A petite blond in a floppy hat and oversize sunglasses strolled by, grasping the hand of a small child. Jacey recognized her immediately: Kate Hudson. A few paces behind her, a burly bodyguard kept watch. The message was clear: DO NOT APPROACH.

Jacey frowned. Being so famous you had to bring a bodyguard to the beach was less than enticing. Jacey's posse was all the protection she ever wanted to need. Well, those of them who weren't pissed off at her, anyway.

"Is this a private moment, or would you care for some company?" Dash asked, interrupting her reverie.

Aja was with him. The boys, one tall and reedy with a concave chest, the other curly-topped and borderline buff, were in bathing trunks with towels slung over their shoulders and beach chairs tucked under their arms. Dash was also carrying an overflowing tote.

Jacey patted the sand next to her.

"I come bearing sunscreen, O Goddess of Malibu," Dash teased. "We can't risk your skin getting all sunburned and blistered, can we?"

"What would I do without you?" Jacey asked, sitting up so Dash could slather her with SPF 45.

"We brought cold drinks and snacks," added Aja, motioning toward the tote bag.

Jacey glanced at it—a bunch of glossy tabloids were sticking out of the top.

"Hot off the press," Dash conceded. "Delivered to our door by a messenger of your friendly agent. So you wouldn't see them on the supermarket shelves first."

"And the last time I was *in* a supermarket would be . . . ?" Jacey challenged in her best diva voice.

"Best you hear what they're saying from us," Aja said.

Jacey groaned. "Could you find a better way to ruin my one day off?"

"It isn't all bad," Dash said. "It's actually kind of funny."

"Funny ha-ha, or funny make-me-cry?"

"You make the call." Dash pulled one of the mags out of the tote.

Jacey drew up her knees and rested her chin on them. She knew the tabs must have had a field day now that they'd sniffed out *Fall from Grace* and were finally able to get photos of her in costume—which they'd use *so* out of context. She braced herself for the onslaught of headlines.

"Jacey—A Slut?!"

"America's Sweetheart Trashes Her Image!"

"Jacey Goes to the Dark Side—Corrupted by Hollywood?"

"Generation Next *Winner Betrays Her Fans!"*

Dash and Aja were snickering as they read the headlines in deep, sonorous voices.

"Wait," Jacey stopped them, remembering Cinnamon's warning. The whole betraying-her-fans thing was the blogger's territory. Now the magazines had picked up on it? "How'd I betray my fans?"

"You don't want to know," Aja said.

"Just read the article, please."

Dash obliged. "We voted for a wholesome young actress, who embraces our all-American values, not one who plays a Goth freak who kicks a great family to the curb only to wind up homeless and pregnant, and doesn't even redeem herself in the end." He looked up at her and wrinkled his perfect nose. "What? It shocks you that they didn't understand the play?"

It kinda did, actually.

"There's even a Jacey-O-Meter," noted Aja, trying to make it sound ridiculous. "To measure fan reaction to the play—they've asked readers to text their feelings. It goes from *A silly lark for Jacey* to *This is Jacey's real personality*."

"What's it at?" Jacey asked.

"It's tipping toward the dark side, if you really want to know," Aja said. When she frowned, he said, "C'mon, Jace—this is funny-ridiculous! Pretend you're a fan reading this. Wouldn't you just roll your eyes and treat it like the lunacy it is?"

I might, Jacey thought. Someone like Desi, a true believer in this stuff—like millions of fans—would probably take it seriously.

Just then, a door slammed, followed by the frantic sound of flip-flops running in the sand. Desi was shouting, waving her cell phone in the air. "Jacey! Jacey! You did it! You got it!"

"What'd I get?" Jacey asked warily.

"What do you think?" Desi was panting from her sprint down the beach. "The nomination, girlfriend! You got the Teen Choice Award nomination!"

"Excellent! I guess not *all* my fans feel betrayed!"

Dash jumped to his feet and grabbed Desi's phone.

"It's right here, a text message from Cinnamon. *Tell J. she got nom. FABULOUS! Call me NOW!*"

"It's on your phones, too," Desi explained, still out of breath, "but you guys left them in the house. Isn't this, like the greatest day ever? You are so the breakout star! You deserve this!"

"Not according to today's tabloids . . ." Jacey trailed off.

"Oh, them." Desi waved them off. "They don't always get it right."

"Wow . . . well, okay, then! *Yes!*" Jacey hooted. "*Yessss!!*" She hugged Desi, Dash, and Aja tightly. She'd followed her heart and her instincts, and it'd come out all right, despite trash-talking tabs and the bothersome blog. How very, *very* cool.

"You really wanted it, didn't you?" Ivy had strolled out to join them.

"Yeah, Ives, I guess I did." She was actually surprised at how thrilled she felt just then. It had been easy to put the whole thing out of her mind when she was preoccupied with the play. Would she have been disappointed if she hadn't been nominated? Devastated, maybe?

"Ummm," Ivy pressed her lips together. "So, acclaim is a good thing," she said meaningfully. "Fame can be fulfilling."

Jacey fumbled for an answer. "It was voted on by teens all over the country, the same people who voted for me during *Generation Next*."

"Come on," Ivy said, "just admit it. You love the adulation you get as wholesome Jacey, winner of *Generation Next*. But you also want quirky, unsympathetic indie parts—dirty-girl roles."

"Can't I have both?" Jacey was starting to feel defensive.

"At your age? In this town? Get real. You're not Julia Roberts. You're not Reese Witherspoon."

"That's so unfair!" Desi's back was up in Jacey's defense. "She's so much younger than they are—she's just starting out."

"Hel-*lo*! My point, exactly. You have to earn the right to have both, Jace."

"Is that what Cinnamon told you?" Jacey challenged.

Ivy's phone rang. She checked the caller ID. "Speaking of. It's Cinnamon, for Jacey."

"Put her on speaker," Jacey requested.

Cinnamon was in overdrive. Between her motor mouth, the low roar of the ocean, and the crackling of the wind in the cell phone, it was hard to catch every word. But Jacey heard the important ones. "Got what we wanted, Breakout Star . . . blunt the effect of the play . . . if we win. No way will [unintelligible] other newcomers get it. . . . You battle it out with Kate."

"Kate . . . who?" Beckinsale, Bosworth, Winslet, Moss, Holmes, Hudson, the is-she-anorexic Kate, or the has-she-gained-weight Kate? And of course—

"Summers," the beachside quintet—Jacey, Ivy, Dash, Desi, and Aja—chorused. Kate Summers, one of Jacey's costars in *Four Sisters*. Of course, she'd be the only Kate in the breakout star category.

Maybe that was why she'd been hammered *and* hostile at the opening-night party. Maybe she had already known she'd be competing with Jacey at the Teen Choice Awards.

"Does Kate have a shot?" Dash yelled into the phone Jacey was holding. "Jacey's a much better actor, and way more famous."

"Not always . . . good," Cinnamon's choppy-sounding responses continued. "Kate . . . has a slimy manager, not above being underhanded."

"And I have you." Jacey meant to be jokey, but it didn't come out that way.

Getting the nomination had tripped a switch. The people who had disapproved of her recent choices—Cinnamon, Guy, Ivy, and Adam—were now the amped-up captains of her cheering squad. Congratulations came via phone calls, e-mails, IMs and text messages. Cinnamon's agency sent flowers; Peyton's PR firm sent a gift certificate for a superluxe spa; Guy Landsman's studio delivered a swaglike gift basket.

Adam Pratt left a typical message: *"I told you so!"*

Only in Hollywood, Jacey thought. Would she ever get used to the duplicity, two-facedness, and fair-weather-friends aspect of it? When she did, she thought ruefully, it'd be time to go home.

Her real friends were truly excited for her, as were her parents, her aunt—Ivy's mom—and others from back home. Emory Farber was thrilled, and so, in his way, was Matt Canseco, who'd texted her: *Interesting news, Dimples. Congrats.*

Ivy was chauffeuring her to the theater the following night when it occurred to Jacey that *she* ought to be congratulating someone, too. She took out her Sidekick and started to type.

"Who're you writing to?" Ivy glanced over.

"Kate—to congratulate her."

Ivy's eyebrows arched. "Why?"

"She deserves the nomination, too. We were in the same movie, and we both nailed our characters."

"Again, why? Acting like the bigger person?" Ivy guessed, rolling her eyes.

"I'm not acting, I mean it. I'm not saying I want her to win, but there's no reason not to congratulate her."

"You should be writing to Cinnamon, you know, kissing her Manolo'd feet for getting you this far. I mean," Ivy said, "think about it. Cinnamon played the game really well."

"Meaning, she played me and Landsman?" Jacey speculated.

"Even though she disagreed with your choices, she did manage to outmaneuver the head of a major studio *and* nab you the nomination."

Jacey was silent. Did Ivy *really* believe that Cinnamon had had anything to do with the voting? Or was this just a way to back into the conversation she really wanted to have? The one where Jacey agreed to do what Cinn—and Ivy—wanted. And they all knew what that was.

"Think about Tobey Maguire," Ivy pressed on. "George Clooney, even Christopher Reeve, may he rest in peace; they all played superheroes. Jessica Alba's kicking butt in the Fantastic Four movies. Even when Halle Berry and Jennifer Garner's hero movies tanked, it hardly killed their careers or their cred."

"I hear you," Jacey allowed, "But Ives . . . can we put this whole thing on pause for a while? Let me finish the run of the play, do the Teen Choice Awards—and then I promise you, we'll talk more and . . ." She halted, looking into her cousin's hopeful green eyes. "We'll find a way to work it out."

Ivy pulled up to the Hole-in-the-Wall Theater. She leaned over and smoothed Jacey's hair affectionately. "It's been a confusing time, I know. But I also know that you have the best heart, little cousin, and the best soul. I won't say another word about it, if you promise you'll think about it seriously. And remember, if you say yes, you can use all that newfound wealth and power—yeah, that's what it'll be—for good things. You can help people, animals, the environment. Go all Brangelina, wear a bunch of colored ribbons, line your arms with rubber bracelets. Even Matt would be on board with that. Charity is so on trend."

The following week was bittersweet. Everyone around Jacey was buzzed about the nomination, while she got to do what she loved most: act. Best of all, no one was pushing her about anything. But the play was limited run, and that run was about to cross the finish line. It would be over very soon.

And then? A feeling of emptiness came over her. She mentally slapped her own wrist. She had so much to be pumped about. She and Ivy were back on good terms—a huge relief! She was honestly happy for her cousin, who was excited about her potential new career and her sweet boyfriend, Emilio.

It was all good.

That applied to the rest of her friends as well. Dash had enrolled in college—he'd had to decline his acceptance to the University of Michigan when he elected to stay in California. Now he was officially a freshman at UCLA. He was already practicing his "Go, Bruins" chant, which was funny, since Dash was not a sports person. But Aja was. And their relationship was totally deepening. How very cool. Dash had never been in a real relationship back in Michigan, so this was nice.

And little Desi. Jacey was proudest of her. Back home, Desi had to drop out of high school to work. Here in Los Angeles, she was getting her GED and would have her diploma soon. As a bonus, Des had found—okay, not a deep relationship—a fling with the *himbo* surfer boy (whom she, Dash, Ivy, and Aja had secretly dubbed Meaty Mike). Jacey had no idea how he supported himself. When the buff-bodied boy with the low, *low* swim trunks wasn't out on the waves, he and his almost-housebroken puppy, Gladstone, hung at the beach house.

Jacey grinned. They'd all reached this point because of her: the only one who wasn't currently in a relationship. Hmmm . . . could that be why she felt so empty?

That situation, she believed, would change. It was fated. If Matt were there right now, alone with her at that moment, all that spouting about "I'm not that guy" would stop. One long, leisurely kiss would do the trick.

'Cause it was an unbearably romantic Malibu night. The breeze played gently on Jacey's arms, the palm trees waved and fluttered, and she could see the surface of the ocean shine and ripple from her deck. Moonbeams cast an eerie light on the swooping seagulls, giving the birds a spectral glow. It was pretty surreal. And not a creature was stirring . . . not even a paparazzo. There'd be no one to interrupt the sexy scene the two of them could enact. If he had been there.

On a whim, Jacey decided to take a short walk before heading inside. She doffed her shoes and dug her heels into the wet, grainy sand, walking along the natural curve of the beach. Soon Jacey found herself at the rise of dunes that overlooked the cove. Their cove. The one she and Matt had almost made out in. Jacey laughed at herself; she hadn't even been conscious of walking there. What, did she think she could magically conjure him up just because she wished it?

Jacey scampered up the rise, careful not to trip over twigs or rocks or let herself be scraped by bits of brush. As she got closer to the top, she actually thought she heard murmuring. She marveled at the tricks the mind could play. Did she crave Matt Canseco so much that she dreamed him there? Reaching the peak of the rocky rise, she gazed down and saw a what she assumed was a mirage, just like a scene in a movie. Only . . . it was real.

There was an outline of a couple, backlit by the moonlight. Sitting on the sand, locked in each other's arms, they were almost one fused silhouette. Mmmm . . . okay, so she hadn't been hallucinating. There were two lovers down there.

Jacey wasn't sure what made her decide to tiptoe down toward them like the paparazzi, creeping in for a better picture. As she drew closer, she was able to see the shadowy pair a bit better. It wasn't Ivy and Emilio. Even in profile, she could tell that the guy was taller than Emilio and had a head of full, dark, wavy hair. The girl was lean and long-legged. It wasn't Desi. Still, the pair seemed familiar somehow. Then the two really began to go at it. His hands slid beneath her top, her fingertips massaged his shoulders.

The girl murmured something and reclined, pulling him down on top of her. Their lips never separated.

Jacey's heel slipped, and she started to slide down the dunes. Damn! The choice was to break her fall by sitting, or risk rolling headlong down the rise. The noise she made as her butt hit the dirt interrupted the couple. They whipped their heads around to look up at her.

When the girl turned, her long, gossamer hair caught the moonlight just so. Her smile of recognition lit up the night. Carlin.

Then Jacey got a full frontal of the guy's bare chest, broad shoulders, and muscled biceps. His piercing eyes locked on to Jacey's.

Matt Canseco did not smile.

jaceyfan blog

Go, me!

Far be it from me to say, "Told ya so."

Chapter Ten

Be the Moving Target

"That's it! That bee-yotch is out of here!" The next morning, Ivy stomped around the kitchen in her flip-flops, as if each thwack were a smack to Carlin's face.

"How could she *do* that?" Dash looked genuinely perplexed as he wrapped an Ace bandage around Jacey's ankle. "How could *he* do that?"

"If no one else has the guts to do it, I'm kicking her bony ass out. Today," Ivy growled. "Not gonna wait for her to come back from wherever she spent the night. Torching her *stanky* stuff."

"Unless I get there first." Desi balled up her fists.

"Stop!" Jacey was perched on a bar stool at the kitchen counter; her swollen ankle elevated on the one next to it. "You're all overreacting."

"He cheated—" Ivy shrieked.

"He's not my boyfriend. He's my crush." Jacey cut her off, grimacing as Dash dabbed the scrapes on her arms and hands with antiseptic.

"Oh, please. Everyone knows how you feel. She back-stabbed you!" Desi insisted.

"Matt never made any promises to me, and as for Carlin, that she-witch can hook up with anyone she pleases," Jacey said miserably.

"They were in the cove where you and Matt . . ." Ivy trailed off, her point made.

"If they didn't want to get caught, they wouldn't have been so close to the house," said Dash, finishing Ivy's thought.

"They were blocked by the dunes," Jacey mumbled. "They didn't plan on being interrupted."

"Maybe Matt didn't, but I bet Carlin hoped you'd find out," Ivy sneered. "She's so jealous of you. Even if you hadn't stumbled on them, don't you think she would have found another way to flaunt this . . . this . . . whatever it is?"

"Let it go," Jacey heaved a sigh. "They're both single, and it looked more than consensual."

Irony Alert: the voice of reason was Jacey's. The fact

that she could be so calm was due only to the sleep-deprivation haze she was still in. She'd spent the entire night awake, just trying to breathe.

After she saw what she saw, after she spun around so fast that she twisted her ankle, after she fell again rushing down the dunes, getting far away from them as fast as she could . . . after she limped into the house, cut and bruised; turned the shower to scalding; turned her phone off; and pulled the covers over her head, she found she'd lost the ability to breathe.

Ivy had found her the following morning hobbling around the kitchen, trying to down some coffee. Ivy had gotten the others up.

Haltingly, painfully, as Dash tended to her physical injuries, Jacey told them what'd happened.

Jacey said in a monotone, "Kicking Carlin out won't change anything. The damage is done. If she and Matt are hooking up . . ." She trailed off.

"No way they're doing it under your nose! And there's no way Carlin is doing it in your *house*." Ivy was steaming. She'd been suspicious of Carlin from day one; now she felt validated. And enraged.

Desi's phone rang. "It's Matt," she said. "Should I pick up?"

"No!" Ivy snatched the Razr from her. "Sure, he's

calling *you*. You're his friend, his homey."

Back when the two posses—Jacey's and Matt's—had first met, it'd come out that Matt's grandfather lived in Hamtramck, the same Detroit outpost where Desi had lived with her grandmother. Matt had spent summers there when he was a kid. He remained devoted to his pops, put money in the older man's bank account every week, just like Desi, who sent her earnings to help her grandma. Based on that connection, the two had established the kind of instant kinship that the others, who hadn't come from their circumstances, could never understand.

Now Desi squirmed. "He probably just wants to see if you're okay."

"What? You're defending him?" Ivy demanded. "Is he too scared to call her directly?"

"Probably," Dash said.

"I bet he tried," Desi said. "Have you checked your messages?"

Jacey shook her head. She had no interest in anything Matt had to say. He'd told her the truth months ago. He liked being a free agent. He knew she wouldn't be able to deal with it. He'd told her everything she needed to know.

So why hadn't she believed him? Why did it hurt so much now?

★ ★ ★

Jacey limped through her last few performances. Delving into her character's pain was a snap, but she had to dig deep during the third act, when Grace finds peace, redemption, and bliss.

Luckily no one in the audience seemed to notice that anything was off. Only Rob, one of Matt's closest friends, knew what had gone down. He also knew enough to keep quiet unless Jacey brought it up.

She did not. She would not. She was determined to put the entire incident behind her—stash it in her mind's trash bin and hope it would permanently delete itself. By the time she got home the night after it happened, Carlin had already packed up her things and left the Malibu house. No one told Jacey exactly how it had gone down, and she didn't ask. She hoped her friends were right: once the C-witch was out of sight, she'd be out of mind.

It was much harder to get Matt out of her mind. She tried to convince herself that he'd been nothing more than a serious crush and a hot movie-star mentor. Matt was the first guy she'd pursued and not gotten.

Matt obviously felt guilty. He kept trying to reach her, first through Desi, then through Ivy, via Emilio. He should have known better, she thought. As if her friends would pass any messages to her.

The only thing *they* offered was advice: lots of it, all unsolicited.

Desi decided Jacey should start dating; her friend Mike had some friends. . . . Ivy, influenced by Emilio, thought Jacey should strive for closure, contact Matt, get her feelings out, and be done with it. Dash, while driving her home from the penultimate performance of the play, told her, "Stay busy. Keep moving; pain can't hit a moving target. It's the best antidote for a broken heart."

"I don't want to stay busy," had been Jacey's first reaction. Now that the play was just about over, now that any hope of having Matt was crushed, she divulged her true feelings: "I want to—"

"Go home? Go back to Michigan?" Dash guessed— correctly. "Seeing your parents would be a Band-Aid, not a cure. And isn't Logan still in town?"

"Thanks for reminding me of another guy who dumped me."

"Listen to Dr. Dash," he said soothingly. "Stay here. Stay busy. Cinnamon wants you high profile: see and be seen. Stay on the voters' radar."

"What does Cinn want me to do, a cross-country mall tour?" Jacey said acidly.

"You keep in touch with teen voters by staying in the news—for good things," Dash explained, ignoring her derision. "Cinnamon's got a bunch of appearances lined up for you, galas and parties to go to, premieres and—"

"Going out partying? I don't have the strength to pretend I feel great. I don't think so."

"I do. You don't want to have a spare minute up until the awards."

"Why?"

"Because the alternative is to lie around here feeling sorry for yourself, licking wounds you don't even think you deserve to have."

Eventually, Jacey had to admit Dash was right. Especially after she checked her text messages the next day.

Dimples, I'm so sorry you saw that. I never meant to hurt you.

Her eyes clouded, and a predictable lump formed in her throat. She hit DELETE, stuck her chin out, and crossed her arms over her chest. *No, I'm not going to answer. I'm not going to care.*

Dash had been right about Cinnamon's plans. Her agent had been waiting for the play to be over before pouncing. She didn't wait long.

The day after the show ended—Jacey had managed to stay at the closing-night party for half an hour before bolting, terrified of Matt's showing up—Cinnamon and Kia arrived at her door. Kia carried a messenger-bag-with-laptop slung across her chest, tote bags strapped over both shoulders, and shopping bags in her hands. Cinnamon clutched only a tall latte.

"What's all this?" Desi asked, after opening the door. The gang had been playing poker, mostly to keep Jacey occupied.

"This? This is just the beginning." The agent, sleek and smooth in a Vivienne Westwood suit and Roger Vivier heels, swept into the beach house and commandeered the couch. While Kia booted up the laptop, Cinn upended the tote bags, placed the shopping bags on the floor, and asked genially, "Are we ready to campaign?"

"What are *we* running for?" Jacey said sarcastically.

"Choice breakout star, of course. You want that teen vote. Or would you rather Kate Summers snatched it? She's your only real competition."

Jacey opened her mouth, but Cinnamon went on. "Think of this campaign as vote-courting, just the way you did for *Generation Next*. Instead of acting out scenes, in *our* campaign, you're acting cool and confident, like the real breakout star. Like you've already won. You'll be using the press, tabloids, blogs, and paparazzi instead of letting them use you. Studies prove people vote for the star they saw last, or most. Or something." She waved a bracelet-bedecked arm.

"Very true," agreed Dash in an I-told-you-that tone.

"Watch carefully, kiddies," Cinnamon said brightly. "You're about to learn, up close and personal, how this town works, and what the payoffs are when it does. We'll do a two-pronged attack. We'll have you up on billboards and attached to a cool product online. You'll go out and about, to parties and events and promote good causes. But first, Kia, would you do the honors?"

Kia pulled out a magazine they'd brought, and opened to the page with the Slickity Jeans ad. "Hot off the presses," she said, holding it up.

"Oh, cute, Jace! It came out great!" Desi exclaimed.

"Not bad. You look . . . uh . . . wholesome," Dash put in.

Jacey studied herself in the magazine ad. Something was off about it. She checked her hair, makeup, and winking smile. Then the outfit she'd chosen, the top, the heels, the jeans—

"Wait! They airbrushed me!" she yelped, finally figuring it out.

Desi and Ivy grabbed for the magazine. Desi's eyes went wide. "You're right! You look ten pounds thinner in this ad than in real life."

Dash peered over Ivy's shoulder.

"Did you know about this, Cinnamon?" Jacey demanded.

Cinnamon shook her head; not a hair moved. "It wouldn't occur to me to ask. That's what they do with all models."

"At least now there's not that much of a difference between you and Carlin," Desi pointed out, before realizing that that probably wasn't the most diplomatic thing to say.

"You mean, Little Miss I-Can-Wear-Skinny-Jeans! 'Oooh, but a size zero is too big for me'?" Jacey snarled.

"On the upside," Ivy said cheerily, "orders for the jeans are already pouring in—isn't that right, Cinnamon?"

"Yes, and if it's any consolation," her agent continued, "you won't be posing for any more jeans ads. We're taking you to the next level. We'll select one really prestigious, high-profile gig. We're talking nice money, image-appropriate offers only. Something *fabulous*! And it's time, Jacey."

The Hollywood-to-English interpretation was: "I've indulged you, you had your little play fling. It's payback time. It's all good."

Jacey asked Desi to call in for pizza. She was going to need sustenance.

Cinnamon described the offers that had come in for Jacey. The first was a request to be the new face of

Dooney & Bourke handbags. Cinnamon upended one of the shopping bags. Satchels, shoulder bags, totes, clutches, and handbags in eye-popping colors poured out.

"A bribe?" Jacey asked.

"No," Cinnamon laughed, "they sent some samples, in case you hadn't heard of Dooney & Bourke."

"I'm not that familiar with them," Jacey admitted, "but I have my cousin, the Imelda Marcos of bags, right here." It was the first time she'd made a real joke in a week. It felt good.

"You'd pose with their new line," Cinnamon explained. "You'd also get to design your own signature bag. What do you think?"

"Sweet!" Ivy chimed in.

Desi piped up, "Mischa Barton, Lindsay Lohan, and Emma Roberts have all done Dooney & Bourke."

To Jacey, the idea of posing with the bags felt like a Slickity Jeans ad, part two. She wasn't keen on it.

Hanes Underwear was next.

"Look who we've got our Hanes on now," Desi sang. "The one Jennifer Love Hewitt from *Ghost Whisperer* was in?"

"That's the one," Cinnamon said. "They sent samples, too."

Bras, panties, T-shirts, sleepwear, and workout fleece tumbled out of another shopping bag.

"Forget it." Jacey nixed it instantly. "I'm not displaying my body."

"You have an amazing body," Ivy said. "A real girl's body, curves and all. You could be the anti-anorexic look. Which would be a cool statement to your fans. It's very on-trend."

Jacey gave her cousin a look. "The tabloids and blogs would have a field day. I might as well just put a big target on my ass. Can't you see the headlines? JACEY—LAY OFF THE PIZZA! And, DID JACEY GET A BOOB JOB? And if I happen to lose a little weight, or they airbrush me, it'd be JACEY—EATING DISORDER!"

Ivy and Desi disagreed, but Jacey remained emphatic.

Cinnamon cocked her head. "So this is a no? You're sure?"

When the pizza arrived, Jacey tucked into a cheesy, greasy slice. Oh, yeah, she was sure.

"What about 'Got Milk?'" Desi asked, devouring a piece of pepperoni. "She'd look cute with a milk mustache."

"Too played," Cinnamon said. She gingerly picked the cheese off a pizza slice, then grabbed a knife to cut the crust off with. "Everyone's done it."

Next on the list was CoverGirl. They were doing a new

smoky eyes look. "They only use A-list stars like Halle Berry," Cinnamon declared.

Desi and Ivy dived into the cache of makeup the company had sent along.

Jacey considered. Her eyes, huge and ocean-colored, were her best feature. And CoverGirl was a name her fans were familiar with. She put that on her "maybe" list.

"There is one more," Cinnamon said. She'd saved the best for last.

"How would you like to be the dancing iPod girl?"

"Did they send—" Dash began, but Desi had already dug them out: the latest iPod MP3 players with video, Nanos in all colors, and the newest, thinnest Shuffle.

"Isn't the girl in the iPod ads in profile?" Jacey asked. "You don't usually see her face."

"It'll be a new campaign for them," Cinnamon explained. "You'd be dancing, the white buds in your ears, but we'd see your face. They're planning billboards, videos, the works. I think this is the coolest, most cutting-edge offer."

"While remaining wholesome and image-appropriate." Jacey gave voice to what her agent was totally thinking.

"You'd be the first young celebrity for them, a breakthrough—"

"For a breakout star," Dash happily finished the

thought. "You gotta admit, Jace, it works."

The debate began. Jacey mostly stayed out of it. As Cinnamon and Ivy went over the pros and cons, Dash asked how much money Jacey would make, Desi played with the iPods, and Kia stared into space. God, that girl was weird, Jacey thought. Ivy was so much the better assistant. Jacey got up, stretched, and limped into the kitchen for a drink. It still hurt to put pressure on the ankle, but she needed a moment alone to think about the offers.

By the time she rejoined her friends, she'd made a decision. "I'll do either iPod or CoverGirl. You guys choose. But I have one condition. I also want to do a PSA."

"Public service announcement?" Kia, who'd come back to their planet, seemed surprised.

"Anything specific in mind?" Cinnamon asked.

Jacey didn't have a particular cause to champion, just a deepening awareness that using her celebrity—whatever she had of it—to help others was something she'd feel good about. Maybe that was selfish, but she needed to feel good right now.

"As long as you don't adopt a child from a third world country—" Cinnamon shuddered. No one was sure if she was kidding or not.

"I was thinking more along the lines of something for

kids, teens. Maybe an antismoking ad, or Get Caught Reading, or Make-A-Wish. Or helping to raise money for childhood diseases."

"You really want to go there?" Cinnamon asked nervously. "Those can be dark places."

"Maybe I can bring a little light in." Jacey looked straight at Ivy when she added, "Set it up."

jaceyfan blog

This Just In

Jacey kicks Carlin out! In a jealous rage, the spoiled-brat star booted the poor girl out of the beach house—for no reason! Unless it's because innocent Carlin naively went out with a certain movie star Jacey's crushin' on? The one who kicked Jacey to the curb? So, is this the new plan, Jacey? If you can't have him, Carlin can't, either? The least you could have done was give the girl a heads-up: she didn't know you'd get so agro.

Luckily, sweet and talented Carlin has made lots of friends in her short time in Hollywood, and many have come forward to offer their homes until she gets her career going.

Here's another Jacey scooplet: inside word has it that she'll be the new face of iPod. You heard it right! The new ads featuring the dancing diva will be up on billboards any day now. And here's an even hotter little slurp of juice: she turned down a certain undergarment company because she's ashamed of her body.

Chapter Eleven

"It's an Honor Just to Be Nominated" and Other Lies . . . Ooops, Sound Bites

Jacey was everywhere. She couldn't drive down the street without seeing her own eyes peering out from a billboard. She couldn't hit a mall without passing posters of her smiling self, nor flip open an issue of *Variety*, nor go to the YouTube or MySpace home pages without being hit with a barrage of "Vote for Jacey" ads.

Cinnamon had been as serious as a pimple on prom night about this campaign.

Even TV wasn't a Jacey-free zone. There were "Vote for Jacey" plugs on *American Idol*, *Dancing with the Stars*, and even *Extreme Makeover: Home Edition*.

Anywhere that teens were likely to be, anything they'd be likely to see—that's where the media blitz was.

Jacey's home state got (in her opinion) the worst of it. In addition to the flood of ads, pro-Jacey flyers were sent to all the middle and high schools. There wouldn't be anyone between the ages of thirteen and nineteen in all of Michigan who wouldn't be reminded of Jacey's hometown-girl-made-good status. Reason enough to vote for her.

"This makes kids across the state think, If Jacey can be a star, I can, too. I'm not that different from her," deduced Dash.

"Where's it say that?" responded Desi, scrunching her forehead.

"It's subliminal," Ivy explained. "It's planting an idea in someone's head without actually saying it. Like, when you look at a magazine ad, it doesn't say that if you buy this dress, or use this makeup, you're gonna look like Jessica Simpson, or Halle Berry, but the message to your brain is is—buy our product, you'll look like a Hollywood star."

"Aha, so you *did* learn something at college," Dash teased Ivy.

Other messages were more direct: Quotes from Jacey's reviews were plastered beneath the "Vote for Jacey" banners. A sample: *Generation Next got it right: Jacey Chandliss is America's newest star!*

And: *If you want to witness true talent, do not miss Jacey's performance—aintitcool.com* and: *As for luminous newcomer Jacey Chandliss, a star has definitely arrived.*

Those were from the old reviews of her *Four Sisters* performance. But the quote most used was from the play no one had wanted her to do: *Until further notice, Jacey Chandliss is the best new actor of her generation.*

Speaking of people who'd opposed her choice and then conveniently about-faced, studio-dude Guy Landsman composed his own message: *Only once in a lifetime does a Jacey Chandliss come on the scene—beautiful, talented, and Michigan-nice.*

The whole thing was truly cringeworthy. Jacey was tempted to draw mustaches on her posters and be photographed on a MySpace page wearing a "Vote for Pedro" T-shirt.

She was the only one who had a sense of humor about it. Everyone else was taking this campaign *very seriously.* No one wondered if the all-out Jacey blitz was overkill. No one at Camp Jacey worried about backlash.

"People vote for whoever's uppermost in their minds," Cinnamon reminded her. "It's imperative that person be you. End of story."

Still, it embarrassed Jacey that two other nominees,

actresses from *The Golden Compass* and the latest Harry Potter movie, hadn't mounted campaigns at all. Did they not have agents in their corners, or did they not care about winning?

Kate Summers did. Her campaign was all about why Jacey should *not* win. *Jacey Chandliss shouldn't even qualify for Choice Breakout. She already broke out by winning* Generation Next *last year!* her ads blared. *With two movies and a play under her belt, she's not even a newcomer. A vote for Jacey in this category is just wrong. Kate Summers, who debuted in* Four Sisters, *is the real breakout star, and must be your choice.*

"When did Snoopy die and make *her* the underdog?" Ivy fumed.

"She's dissing the nomination process and the TCAs," Dash mused, "but no one will see it that way. She's making Jacey look like the greedy girl who's already on top, while Kate's a deserving up-and-comer."

Cinnamon, when pressed, conceded that the strategy could score for Kate. "Everyone feels for the little guy," she said with an eye roll.

"That's so unfair!" Desi complained. "Let's strike back! There's so much we could say about her. Like, if her IQ was any lower, she'd have to be watered daily."

"Let's leave the celebrity mudslinging to the

professionals. The tabloids will invent a feud without any help from us," Dash reminded everyone.

"Jacey doesn't *do* feuds," Ivy said. "That's not her image."

"That's my point!" Desi exclaimed. "Jacey should win because she's a positive role model, unlike Kate-bake, the poster child for underage drinking."

"We are *not* going there," Jacey declared. "No way."

"Personal attacks are so last November, anyway," Ivy sniffed.

Cinnamon had the final word. "We ignore Kate. We continue to show why Jacey deserves the vote. We keep her face out there."

Team Jacey took that concept and ran with it. To the extreme, you could say. They booked her on the *Today Show*, where she talked to Matt Lauer about overnight stardom. She modeled cute clothes on *Good Morning, Los Angeles!*, played interviewer on *Access Hollywood*, practically drooled over Mark McGrath on *Extra*, jawed with Regis and Kelly, even agreed to a cooking bit with Rachael Ray. The last required the most acting, since the only thing Jacey had ever cooked successfully was chocolate-chip cookies, and that was from a tube.

She got to introduce Fergie, of the Black Eyed Peas, on MTV's *TRL*, which was very cool, and just missed Johnny

Depp backstage at *Entertainment Tonight*! Grrr! She appeared at the opening of the Lucky Brand Jeans store in Beverly Hills and did a radio interview with Ryan Seacrest.

By the end of week one, Jacey had uttered the phrase "It's an honor just to be nominated" so many times she felt like a windup toy, programmed with four phrases that repeated over and over: "I'm so excited to be here!" "I love the Teen Choice Awards!" "All the nominees are so talented!" "I'm honored to be in their company."

To her friends, she wondered aloud, "What if, in the middle of an interview, I get stuck like a broken Talking Elmo and keep saying: 'I'm honored . . . I'm honored . . . I'm honored.'" She let her body go slack, imitating a conked-out toy.

No one thought that was funny. They were busy shuttling her between appearances, making sure she was on time and prepared. Which meant traveling with Yuki, her personal hairstylist; Marcia, makeup artist to the stars; and, most crucial, Irina.

Jacey's stylist was the one who chose what she'd wear for each appearance: a pink taffeta dress for *Good Morning, Los Angeles!*; a leopard print for *Live with Regis and Kelly*; Slickity Jeans and a tank top for Rachael Ray. Wholesome all the way.

Rules of conduct were constantly impressed upon her by publicist Peyton and sanctified by Cinnamon.

Other stipulations: no super-low-cut tops, no teensy miniskirts, no gossiping, and no getting caught chatting with any "controversial" celebrities. That included anyone who'd been in rehab, was rumored to be anorexic, had punched someone in a bar brawl or tossed a drink on someone, received a scolding letter for too much partying, or whose last name was the same as that of a hotel chain. Other than that, she was directed to "Be friendly but vague; smile a lot."

She was to keep it clean on the dance floor—no grinding, suggestive moves, or dancing on tabletops. Always pose for a photographer in a group, never alone with any one guy. If Jacey drank something, it had to be clear liquid. "We can always claim it was water," said Peyton. Jacey ended up drinking nothing stronger than club soda—how else was she going to remember all the rules?

"I feel for you, Jacey, I really do. It's just so tough, being a celebrity," Dash deadpanned when he came into the makeup room at *Regis and Kelly*, "Getting pampered, catered to every minute—that must be so hard!"

Jacey cracked a smile, which caused Marcia to slip and draw a lipstick line up her nostril. Marcia was not amused.

Jacey had to admit that this round-the-clock

self-promotion was fun. All actors like an audience. And being fawned over wasn't too hard to stomach. Bonus: the campaign kept her so busy that there were whole stretches of time when she didn't brood about Matt.

When the sun went down, the merry-go-round picked up speed. Nights were for galas, parties, benefits; see-and-be-seen—in the most positive, wholesome way—events.

Parties blended into one another, a dizzying rush of glitz, glam, and sparkle, of rolling with the Hollywood A-list of celebrities, models, designers, heiresses, sports stars, and their entourages. Jacey and her crew were chauffeured by stretch limo to fabulous mansions, astounding poolside hotels, famous restaurants, even the Pacific Design Center and the J. Paul Getty Museum. And that wasn't even counting the red carpets they walked down for the hottest movie premieres.

They got glam for the Chrysalis Butterfly Ball and an opening of the newest Dolce & Gabbana store (where Jacey felt like an absolute giant posing next to teensy-tiny Mary-Kate and Ashley.)

They got their Nikes on for the Race to Erase MS; she met Michael J. Fox at a benefit to find a cure for Parkinson's disease; she also did the Revlon Run/Walk for Breast Cancer *and* Great Strides for Cystic Fibrosis.

She often crossed paths with her rival, Kate Summers. There were no fireworks, no harsh words exchanged, no one-upping or even snubbing. It was almost as if Jacey and Kate had some kind of unspoken agreement not to acknowledge the competition, even though they were the only two people who could understand what the other was feeling. There were times, even, when Jacey felt bad about the all-out media blitz her people had constructed—and sensed Kate was ashamed of the anti-Jacey ads her side had produced.

Not that the girl ever said as much. Most of the time Kate was too busy working the room, socializing, flirting, gossiping with Sierra—her posse of one!—and hitting the open bar.

Jacey was finding these evening events very different from her daytime self-promotions. She was actually inter-ested in the cause-related benefits. That was a side effect her agent probably hadn't counted on.

Jacey was ashamed to be so ignorant about Darfur and the atrocities that were going on in that region of Africa. While she and her friends were busy mocking stars and their high-profile adoptions, Jacey had never realized how much money they had donated to orphanages and health facilities. She walked away from several events really impressed. Those stars were such tabloid bait—and yet they kept on doing good deeds. That was extremely cool, she thought.

The best moment happened when Jacey found herself in a clutch of people listening to Leonardo DiCaprio talk about the environment, and ecology, and saving our planet's natural resources. Who'd-a *thunk* she'd been more captivated by what Leo said than by how hot he looked, or by the thrill of being inches from him!

She was soon over feeling embarrassed about her ignorance and became determined to join the stars she admired and do something positive. Ivy's words echoed in her brain—words to the effect of, "If you take the deal, if you become a superstar, you can really help others." That could be her trade-off for what Matt called selling her soul.

Not, she reminded herself, that she cared what Matt said. Luckily, there was no danger of running into the heartbreaker at any of these events—or of seeing Carlin. The latter wasn't a big enough star to be invited, and Matt flat out refused to have anything to do with those kinds of scenes. He supported the causes he cared about in his own quiet way. Dressing up and glad-handing, smiling for pictures, giving sound bites to the press, those things were not his way.

Besides, he'd been asked, then told, then warned by her friends to stop trying to apologize to Jacey. The best thing he could do for her was to stay away.

Reporters didn't play by those rules. Ever since the near-kiss shots taken at the cove that night, the tabloids had had a field day with Jacey and Matt's supposed "on-again, off-again" romance. And the "legitimate" press, those actually invited to benefits and parties, weren't above a gossipy scoop.

TV reporter Maria Menounos quizzed her on the exact nature of her friendship with Matt Canseco. And Jacey spoke to Vanessa Minnillo at MTV's Rock the Vote event; Vanessa was looking for an exclusive comment on Jacey's feelings about Matt's running off with the runner-up, Carlin.

Jacey's terse "Matt and I are friends" and "No comment" weren't what any reporter wanted to hear. With smiles, they moved on to other celebrities for juicier scoops.

When the press wasn't on her, other guests were. "It's so brave of her to show her face after the Matt and Carlin thing. Jacey must be devastated," Sierra Tucson sniped at the wingding Jessica Simpson threw for her sister Ashlee.

At the *Grey's Anatomy* DVD celebration, Jacey overheard someone say, "I hear Matt and Carlin broke up. Now Jacey can get him back."

At those awkward, hurtful moments, Jacey just tossed her hair regally and walked away.

It wasn't much consolation for Jacey, but Kate was obviously feeling the pressure, too. It seemed that no one had advised her to lay off the liquor. Maybe she felt like being a rebel. Or worse, maybe Desi was right and Kate had a real problem. Either way, on one regrettable night when a reporter stuck a microphone in her face, the dazed Kate actually threw up on it.

jaceyfan blog

Jacey Fails Fashion 101!

It's Fashion Rehab time! As a public service to all Jaceyfans, here's a roundup of the past few weeks' worth of fashion felonies:

In *Us Weekly*, she lost out to Rachel Bilson and Hilary Duff in the "Who Wore It Best" column for the Christian Lacroix eyelet ruffle dress. Rachel got 49%; Hilary, 43%; and Jacey? A paltry 5%. Ouch. But wait, there's so much more! To wit:

Entertainment Weekly's Style Section said her mini had too many sequins, ruffles are for potato chips, and her jewelry looked like "macaroni."

The Fashion Police also called her out for the striped top she wore on Rachael Ray, saying she looked like an escaped inmate from San Quentin.

E! TV slammed that top, too. "It looked like she'd left it on the grill too long."

In the "When Bad Clothes Happen to Good People" column, Jacey was described as "a flop in a too-tight, too-sequined cocktail mess—er, dress."

In the "What Was She Thinking?" roundup, the pink taffeta was "a perfect dress—for a six-year-old! Were you modeling for Ballet Barbie?" And, of her long bangs, "Some girls *want* a Shetland pony. Jacey looked like one."

OK! magazine went with empathy, using the title of the famous song "So You Had a Bad Day," calling her sparkling ensemble "Tinker Bell goes Goth."

ET's Cojo carped, "If heinous were a color, that's what I'd call starlet Jacey Chandliss's dress on the red carpet last night. And that leopard-print schmatta? Back to the jungle, or the old folks' home in Miami Beach. Oh, honey! Take a hint: maybe those around you don't have your back—but are putting a knife in it instead. Ditch the stylist and fire your gay friend for letting you out of the house like this!"

And in the phony-baloney battle for Alpha Teen—I hear Kate's got it locked up already. I certainly hope so—even I, your trusty blogger, agree that both she and Jacey deserve to be on this list: Top Ten Celebrities We're Sick Of!

Chapter Twelve

It Happened in Vegas . . .

"Viva Las Vegas! We're goin' to Vegas!" Ivy's grating, off-key singing did nothing to help Jacey's pounding headache. It was Sunday afternoon, her first real break from blitz-full weeks of posing, partying, pumping the flesh, manipulating the press, and being trashed for her fashion flubs. "Exhausted, overwhelmed, and stung" described her mood.

Ivy had just returned from meeting with Cinnamon to review the publicity campaign. "Upbeat and energetic" described *her* mood.

"Who's going to Vegas?" Jacey mumbled, hunting for an asprin in the downstairs bathroom.

"I'll go!" Desi raised her hand enthusiastically.

"All of us," Ivy beamed cheerfully. "Four first-class tickets await at the airport."

"Why?" Dash asked warily.

"When?" Jacey asked as she gulped water to wash down the found aspirin.

"Why ask why? Soon!" Ivy, exuberant, teased.

"Omigod, Las Vegas!" Desi squealed. "For real, Ives? We're going?"

"Jacey and her guests have been invited to attend the VIP preopening of Glam Slam, a new group of swank designer boutiques at the Palms Hotel and—this is the cool part—it's being held at Fever, only the most elite nightclub on the Strip," Ivy explained merrily.

"The Strip?" Dash's eyebrows arched. "You've already switched to Vegas-tongue?"

"We are talking *megaparty*, people, the likes of which even *we* have not seen!" Ivy babbled on. "We all get free clothes and accessories—each from a different designer or boutique—excellent swag bags, and best of all? The only photographers allowed will be from *Vegas Magazine*, *Elle*, *InStyle*, and *Teen Vogue*. No paparazzi! No annoying press asking nosy questions. No bad-mouthing what we do or wear. Translation: this is a free ride to sin city. We can wear what we've never dared, be as wild as we wanna be . . . 'cause what happens in Vegas stays in Vegas!" She finished with a flourish, eyes flashing.

"What do they expect from Jacey?" Dash asked suspiciously. "What does she have to do?"

"Nothing," Ivy crowed. "A snapshot or two with some hot designers—c'mon, guys, we're talking Marc Jacobs! Stella McCartney! Zac 'Freakin' Posen! That's *it*! Her glorious, Jace-ified presence snags us all an unforgettable experience where anything goes!"

"Anything goes for *you* guys," Jacey put in. "I'll probably have to smile a lot and try to look wholesome, happy, and sober, while you guys can play, flirt, get trashed, and gamble. Just like the past few weeks."

"No!" Ivy insisted. "You're not getting it, Cuz. This isn't part of the Teen Choice campaign. This is a bonus! Extra! Extra! A juicy soiree that happened our way. Nothing you do will show up in the tabloids, and, since it's out of town, it probably won't even land in the blog. Cinnamon promises you can let loose at this one." Ivy draped her arm around Jacey. "You deserve it. And you have my sworn promise, no one will bug you, pressure you, or guilt you into anything. C'mon, everyone who's anyone, fashion icons *and* Hollywood A-listers, will be there. This is gonna rock the Casbah!"

A few days later, Jacey curled up in a window seat of the

first-class cabin of an American Airlines jet and clamped on noise-blocking headphones. She wanted no part of the heated argument between a testy Ivy and a defensive Desi. It had started at the terminal; they carried it on to the plane.

In a patented "Oh, no, you *di*-int!" Desi move, the curly girl had cashed in her first-class ticket for two coach seats: one for her, one for Meaty Mike.

Ivy railed, "How could you? That's cheating!"

Desi wailed back, "You *said* we could cut loose. What's the problem? Emilio will be there. Aja will be there. Why can't I have someone, too?" She latched on to Mike's bulging bicep. He looked indifferent, like he'd rather have been catching a wave.

"Emilio and Aja got their own *invitations*. Mike—" Ivy turned to him. "No offense, it's not personal—Mike did not. It's . . . it's . . ." she stammered, "not done."

"And yet, it appears done," Dash said wearily. "Let it go."

Ivy could not. "You should have asked first."

"I knew it'd be cool with Jacey," said Desi, sticking her chin out. "I know her better than you do."

Dash played peacemaker, keeping the argument from escalating, and keeping Jacey out of it by squiring her directly on to the plane. She tried not to think about the fact that if Emilio and Aja had gotten invitations, Matt probably had received one, too. The last few hectic weeks had afforded her whole half-hours when she didn't think about him and several good stretches when she didn't find herself picturing him with Carlin, either.

But if Matt showed up . . . ?

Matt. Fashion. Vegas.

Nah. Ivy would have told her.

Jacey gazed out the window, remembering the last time she'd been airborne. It hadn't gone so well. She'd chartered her own plane, racing back to Michigan to make it in time for her high school prom. It was an over-the-top move that she'd lived to regret.

The Bloomfield Hills High School graduating seniors had either resented her being there—"The Hollywood star, the diva, is here," they'd sniped—or bombarded her with questions. The sole reason she'd taken such extreme measures to get there had been to reconnect with her then-boyfriend, Logan. She'd been with the basketball star–slash–valedictorian for two years, but at the time hadn't seen him in two months, which had seemed an eternity to both of them.

After all that, they never got a moment of privacy. There'd been no reconnecting, let alone romance; nothing even came close to the love scene Jacey had scripted in her head. They did kiss—finally. But Jacey'd felt nothing. Neither had Logan. He had made it clear, without words, that she'd lost her place in his heart.

Worse—in retrospect—was the fact that she hadn't had time to see her parents during that quick trip back. They had been mad at her, and sad for her.

They still were.

This time, though, they were upset about the beating Jacey was taking from the weekly celeb magazines, the tabloids, and the blog.

Her mom was furious about pretty much everything, from her daughter's being trashed by the self-appointed Fashion Police to the drubbing Jacey continued to get from the blogger, and every tabloid-tattler and Web site in between.

"You should demand a retraction," her mom insisted. "You shouldn't have gotten only five percent of the vote. You looked beautiful! Those other girls are lovely, but they're too skinny!"

"If I ever find out who that creep blogger is," her step-dad swore, "I'll come out there—I will—and give him a piece of my mind! The nerve of that imbecile, to write those awful things about you!"

Her parents had gotten their vent on for close to an hour—hence, the headache she'd been left with when Ivy came dancing in with their Vegas invites.

Cece Chandliss Taylor and Larry Taylor weren't usually this stressed, but because Jacey was out and about so much (a ploy that kept Jacey top-of-mind with voters) she was also a constant target for the tabloids.

"Mom, you can't let it upset you," Jacey had said when her stepdad hung up. "You're pregnant; you shouldn't be having any negative thoughts."

"Doesn't it hurt you, honey, all the stuff they write about you?" her mom had asked softly.

At that moment, Jacey visualized her mom's eyes welling up. Her own did the same. She tried to lie. "I've learned to ignore it."

But she wasn't that great an actress. Her mom saw right through her, even from 2,000 miles away. "Honey, is this all worth it?" she asked.

That was a question Jacey was still asking herself.

"Why are all these girls flashing their boobs?" Desi was perplexed; Mike was wide-eyed.

The posse—plus one—were nearing the Palms, heading for the VIP entrance that led directly to the penthouse party. It was roped off and guarded by a pair of burly bouncers who looked threatening enough to break the camera of any paparazzo who dared come too close. Not a lensman was in sight—just dozens of girls, clamoring to gain entry, pressing against the ropes. The girls were so desperate to get in it was like they were trying to get beads at Mardi Gras. They were baring breasts, cajoling, and offering bribes so the bouncers would open the rope and let them in.

"Is this what they do here?" Ivy wondered aloud. "What happened to paying off the doormen like everywhere else?"

"We're not in Kansas anymore, Dorothy," Dash deadpanned. "I'm not even sure what planet we're on."

As the limo doors opened, the crowd turned and rushed the car, shouting, "It's Leo!" "It's Tyra!" "It's Donatella!" "It's Dave Navarro!" "It's . . ." Then, disappointed, many mumbled, "It's nobody."

Jacey was taken aback. That was the first time she'd been called "nobody" in a year. It felt . . . weird.

"They mean nobody who can help them get in," Dash leaned closer to explain.

"Is getting into a party worth humiliating yourself for?" Jacey asked, as she and her friends were ushered past the desperate babes.

As it turned out? Well . . . yeah.

Admittedly (albeit shamefully), it was worth doing almost anything just to gawk at the scene. The sign in the elevator was a clue: LEAVE YOUR CAMERAS AND INHIBITIONS AT THE DOOR.

Jacey, Dash, Ivy, and Desi, along with Meaty Mike, stepped out of the elevator and onto—Mars? It sure felt like the red planet. The enormous circular interior was done in murals and mirrors. It was a swirling frenzy of fiery reds, sunburst oranges, and blinding yellows. A girl could lose her balance just trying to take it all in—especially if she was, like Jacey, already teetering in her Stella McCartney T-strap high-heeled sandals.

Fever was aptly named—it was dizzyingly hot. A slender-stemmed champagne glass filled with bubbly was placed in Jacey's hand the moment she arrived. You didn't even need the music to feel the pulsating vibe—and later that night, the beats would be live: the Killers were performing!

And you didn't need the eye-popping bumper-to-bumper crop of celebrities, fashionistas, trendsetters, designers, morose models, and trust-fund Tinker Bells to feel as if you had wandered into the cantina scene from, no, not *Star Wars*, call it *Bling Wars*.

An SAT word popped into Jacey's head. *Phantasmagoria*: a series of fantastical images, somehow related, usually in a dream. That was what Fever felt like.

"There's Tim Gunn!" squealed Desi, dropping Mike's

arm to rush over to the silver-haired star of *Project Runway*. The distinguished-looking host was surrounded by designers from the previous season's show. And bonus! Heidi Klum and Seal were there. If Jacey had *really* left her inhibitions at the door, she'd have cut in front of Desi to rush them. She was totally addicted to that show.

Clusters of beautiful people were everywhere—at tables, on the dance floor, on S-shaped love seats that were placed strategically around the room. Many guests were passing around bottles of Patron tequila and tossing back shooters. There was plenty of chatting, laughing, cuddling, and, in a few cases, some serious canoodling.

And . . . splashing? Where was that water coming from?

"Is that . . . what I think it is?" asked Dash, decked out in a smart Zegna suit and Prada Sport loafers, as he twirled Jacey around. An actual waterfall, cleverly tucked under a circular stairway, cascaded into a bubbling Jacuzzi tub. Several sloshed—and now soaked—guests were already taking a dip.

"A hot tub in the middle of a nightclub!" Dash exclaimed.

"Told ya,'" Ivy boasted, quaffing her champagne. "This is not the same-old same-old. The stairway goes to Heaven—a media room. It's got TV, PlayStations, poker tables, slot machines, private rooms for massage, a steam room, and a sauna."

"How 'bout a coed sauna?" They recognized the voice—Emilio's.

Ivy was psyched. "Hey, I didn't know you were here yet."

"You look awesome," Emilio whistled, checking her out. Ivy wore a stunning ivory-beaded Dior minidress, paired with high platform heels. The green-eyed girl was a knockout.

Ivy actually blushed and, for once, couldn't think of anything to say. Finally she went with, "I hardly recognize anyone, do you?"

"It's the superstars of the fashion crowd—designers, models, stylists, Vegas A-listers," Emilio explained. "We're the nobodies in this crowd."

"So I've been told," Jacey chuckled.

"Wait—it gets better. Been to the ladies' room yet?" Emilio asked.

"Should I?" Jacey asked.

"Only if you *don't* really have to go—there's a long line for the unisex bathrooms, and no line at all for the—"

"Men's?" Ivy guessed, interrupting her man.

"Mere humans are restricted to the unisex. Then there's the VIP bathroom. Which, sorry to say, even Jacey doesn't qualify for," Emilio explained.

"You're kidding, right?" Ivy asked.

"Nope. Huge brawls have broken out over people try-ing to use it, or cutting the line for the unisex. It's really funny."

Jacey shook her head. The levels to which elitism rose still amazed her. I'm better than you, so I get to pee in a special bathroom? Insane! "Okay, so what other nobodies are here?" she asked, looking around.

"The usual suspects," Emilio said, ticking off a bunch of young Hollywood stars. "From our crowd, Rob and Gina are here. Aja's looking for you, Dash. And I think your agent sent her assistant—Kia, is that her name? And last, but never least, Kate Summers and Sierra Tucson. Your competition and her uni-posse are by the bar. Guess who they're talking to?"

Jacey glanced over to the spot where Kate, in a strap-less, belted mini, and Sierra, sparkling in silver, were chat-ting up two well-heeled older guys.

"The sleazeball in the navy suit? That's Kate's man-ager," Emilio explained. "The other one? Wearing the red tie? He's from the Teen Choice Awards board. Wanna bet something not so kosher is going on?"

"Emilio, stop, don't make her crazy," Ivy commanded. "Cinnamon will find out what goes down tonight—if any-thing does go down."

"Is Matt—?" Jacey started to ask, when she felt a tap on the shoulder. Her heart pounding wildly, she spun around—and came face to face with . . . not Matt, but a lovely Fever hostess, who said, "I'm sorry to disturb you, Jacey, but Ms. McCartney would like to meet you."

Jacey's jaw dropped. "Stella McCartney wants to meet *me*? Are you sure?"

"You're wearing Ms. McCartney's ensemble. She's curious to see how it works on you," the hostess explained.

Jacey gulped. She'd picked the outfit because she'd fallen for the top, a backless halter in a frisky leopard print that matched the shoes. Never in a million years had she imagined that Stella McCartney—famous designer and daughter of the legendary Beatle Paul—would summon her.

She clung to Dash and whispered, "You have to come with me!"

As they followed the hostess over to the cozy sofa where the apple-cheeked designer was holding court, all Jacey could think was, *This is so Desi . . . but would it be, like, the most cheesy thing in the world if I asked for an autograph for my mom? She's the hugest Beatles fan.*

It wasn't because Jacey lost her nerve that she didn't ask, only that as soon as she got there, the group of people around Stella—who were all so nice and friendly!—

began chatting excitedly. They examined the top and the matching pants Jacey had on, making suggestions, hoisting the halter up a little, and bringing the back down even further.

"It's one of her first designs that a shorter person can wear," one of them whispered, offering Jacey a shot glass of tequila. "She's very excited about it."

"Me too," agreed Jacey, tossing her head back and sending the scorching liquid down her throat. Instantly, she began to cough; her eyes watered. Whoa! Jacey had never had tequila before. She didn't think she'd be back for seconds.

A photographer from *Elle* magazine asked for a picture, and Stella posed with Jacey, who totally came off looking like some starry-eyed fan.

Dash, who'd been watching, laughed. "You were so cool . . . *not!*"

Playfully, she punched him in the arm. "Text Cinnamon to contact Stella's agent—my mom would die if I got her an autograph. This is so special."

It really was. The more Jacey and Dash mingled, the more they recognized other superstars of the fashion world. Gwen Stefani was promoting her L.A.M.B. label off in a VIP corner. Sean John's Diddy was also in the house— in an even more secluded, roped-off VIP area.

Dash had finally spotted Aja and left to join him. Desi popped over with a yummy-looking hors d'oeuvre. Mike trailed behind, hoisting a plate piled high with unfamiliar-looking finger food.

"Dude!" the surfer exclaimed, "you gotta try this." He held what looked like a lobster claw covered with crumbs and salt.

"What is it?" Jacey asked, tentatively taking it from him.

"It's a pretzel-crusted lobster," Mike said. "It rocks!"

The tender lobster meat was soft and juicy, and the crust was a surprising inspiration. "What else is here?" she asked, eyeing the plate of exotic appetizers.

"No idea, but I'm getting more."

"Wait, we know what this is," Desi said, picking up a round minibun topped with a half-dollar-sized hamburger. "It's a Kobe beef burger," she said, as the juices dripped down her chin, "named for Kobe Bryant, the basketball star."

Jacey started to laugh and was about to correct her, but just then, Mike took a cocktail napkin and gently dabbed Desi's chin clean.

"Mmmm . . . it's so tender," Desi said, licking her lips.

So tender. Jacey could not have put it better. She might have added, so intimate. It was an intimate and tender gesture.

Just like that, she understood what Desi saw in Meaty Mike. So what if he wasn't the brightest bulb on the Christmas tree? He was a nice guy, loyal as a lapdog, and *so* sweet to her.

That counted.

Another band ramped up out by the DJ booth. Desi dragged Mike and Jacey onto the crowded dance floor. All three got with their karaoke, singing along as they danced.

A waitress bearing a tray of tequila shooters passed by. On a whim, Jacey threw back another. As soon as her watery eyes cleared up, an electric warmth radiated through her body. She threw her hands up in the air, shook her hips, and grooved to the music. There were so many awesome people moving together on the dance floor!

A slick guy in a pink shirt and tie, looking confidently impressed with himself, sidled up to her. His line was so lame: "I don't know you, but I'd like to."

Jacey smiled, but didn't encourage him. He wasn't deterred, though.

"I'm Harry," he said a bit louder, over the music. "And you are—?"

"Hermione." Jacey had no idea what had come over her.

"Her-*what*?" Harry asked, leaning in closer.

"Her-*my*-oh-nee." She pronounced it slowly, clearly.

He was clueless, but persistent. "My dad owns the hotel," he told her. "Seriously."

"My dad's a Muggle," Jacey said, just as seriously.

"No kidding . . . well . . . uh, hope you're having fun." Hapless Harry gave up and danced away.

"Toodles," Jacey waved as she continued to dance.

"You're bad." Dash said over his shoulder. He was dancing with Aja now.

"You mocked him just because he didn't recognize you?" Aja guessed.

Dash tipped her chin up with a finger and looked into her eyes. "How many drinks have you had? You seem tipsy."

"No mocks, that was banter you overheard," she said defensively. "Besides, is it asking too much for someone to have a passing familiarity with Harry Potter? C'mon."

"Your snob is showing," Dash said. "I doubt Meaty Mike reads J.K."

"M.M. gets a pass. Other fine attributes are at work there."

Aja pulled her into a dip, and the three of them laughed at how goofy they were acting in this rock-*tastic* nightclub filled with fabulous fashionistas. Being in a paparazzi-free zone was a major attitude adjuster. They had gone from wary to carefree and from tense to chill. Ah, the freedom to be doofy, look silly, blurt out whatever came to mind. To be *normal*. She'd missed it.

Jacey was so relaxed she didn't even make a caustic comment when her next dance partner, Adam Pratt, cut in. She grinned, "Hey, *Galaxy* boy, how's it hangin'?"

"I'm so relieved you're here," Adam said as he rocked out to the Black Eyed Peas classic "Let's Get It Started." "I barely recognize a soul. It's intimidating with all these models around."

"Adam Pratt, intimidated by models? Don't all guys lust after those beautiful, bony babes?" Jacey teased.

"Not me."

"Why?"

"They're all too tall!" Adam snorted, "unlike you, my little Choice Breakout ladybug."

Jacey laughed. That was more like the Adam she knew . . . and sometimes detested. Though it suddenly hit her that there were many people higher on her Hollywood-detest list than Adam. He actually had some good qualities.

"In case you didn't recognize it," Adam said proudly, "I'm wearing an Eskander cashmere sweater. It cost thousands. But it's worth it; it's so soft—here, feel." He took her hand and placed it on his heart.

O-kay, she thought, quickly removing her hand from the creamy gray fabric. Adam was a deeply superficial, social-climbing publicity hound. But at least he just put himself out there, didn't pretend to be anything else. He got credit for that in Jacey's book. He was no master actor, but he *was* a really good dancer. Smooth, fluid, great rhythm. Unlike Matt, who danced as if he were having a seizure. She'd once found that really sweet.

The camera loved Adam, but physically, he didn't do it for her, not the way other guys did. Matt was dark and ropy; Logan had been tall, broad-shouldered, and athletically handsome. There was something wispy about Adam: the fine blond hair, styled to look shaggy-casual; the oblong face; the freckled, milky coloring; the straight nose; the light brown, impassive eyes; the thin lips.

"Did you write your acceptance speech yet? I hear Kate has. . . ."

And then, the things that came out of those lips. Not so appealing.

Jacey shook her head no.

"What are you waiting for?" Adam pressed. "It's ten days away. Want me to help you? I'm really good at acceptance speeches."

"Was that your major in film school?"

"Snaps, Chandliss! Just for that, I'm gonna twirl

you. . . ." He grabbed her hand and expertly set her spinning in front of him. His quick, deft move took her by surprise.

". . .Within an inch of your cute little life, twirly-girl," Adam finished triumphantly.

He kept twirling her; she got dizzy, and the room sped by. Everyone looked blurry: Dash, Aja, Desi, Mike, and a hot, dark-haired guy whose name wasn't coming to her. Adam kept spinning her—and she saw more of the hot guy each time she went around. He was ensconced on a love seat, surrounded by a crowd, while being cuddled by a group of girls—a buxom blond, a dark-haired beauty, and . . . was that Kate Summers?

"Adam, stop, I'm dizzy."

"That's the point," he chortled.

"No, no, I'm seeing things that aren't there. Wait a sec."

Adam stopped, and Jacey took several long calming breaths. Okay, she wasn't going to pass out. Or throw up. Now, as for that blur . . .

Matt had cleaned up well. Surprisingly, that was her first thought. He'd traded torn jeans and tight T-shirts for black trousers and a crisp white button-down, over which his leather jacket hung open.

Chapter Thirteen

. . . Ended Up on Real-Time Streaming Video

Ivy. Jacey needed Ivy. Now. Assuring Adam she'd be right back, she flew around the crowded room looking for her, weaving through clusters of models, outrageously dressed designers, and giddily plastered starlets. She consciously avoided the section where Matt was camped.

Ivy was nowhere to be found, but Desi was. Her petite pal pointed toward Heaven, the upstairs media room. Jacey tried to take the circular staircase two steps at a time, but the combination of high heels and tequila rendered that impossible.

Ivy was in the middle of a poker game when Jacey wrenched her away.

"Sorry to interrupt," she muttered. "I need you to see

something." She dragged Ivy to the staircase, leaned over the railing, and pointed downward.

"What's he *doing* here?"

Ivy paused. "He wasn't supposed to go downstairs. I thought you wouldn't see him."

"You knew he was here? And you didn't tell me?"

"He wasn't supposed to come. He said he wasn't, but then he just hopped in the car with Emilio at the last minute. By then it was too late to tell you."

"I assume he knows I'm here," Jacey said.

"Probably."

"Why is he here, then? He's been avoiding me, just like we asked him to. Which is what we want."

"Oh, Jacey," Ivy said gently, shaking her head. "Not everything's about you, sweetie, remember? And if you can't figure out why he's here, you haven't been listening to me. This is Las Vegas. There are . . . I hate to say this . . . girls to whom hooking up with a movie star is a major accomplishment. There's gambling, booze, and his posse is all here. Matt is twenty-one. Legal, single—and a player."

Jacey pressed her lips together hard. Her lip gloss tasted sour, like tequila.

"Maybe you should see him in action, firsthand," Ivy said softly. "Maybe then you'll stop trying to believe he's something else. I'm sorry."

Ivy was not nearly as sorry as Jacey was for herself. Ivy had found a good guy, a true guy; so had Desi. And she—the star, the beauty, the best actress of her generation, a contender for Choice Breakout—had been dumped and kicked to the curb, by not one, but two guys in the last six months. Was there something about her that repelled the guys she wanted and attracted only the nonstarters like Adam and that Harry jerk on the dance floor?

No.

Suddenly determined, she made her way back down the steps. How 'bout she didn't go all pity-city for a change?

Having nowhere to go, the self-pity turned into screw-it-all fury. She grabbed hold of Adam and announced, belligerently, "Come on, Pratt boy, *lemme* show ya how we kick it in the Motor City!"

Adam's face registered surprise, but he just said, "Bring it."

Did she ever. The live music had given way to a DJ, who cranked out dance grooves. An oldie was playing now, but it was perfect for her mood. The song was "Footloose."

Jacey led Adam to the middle of the dance floor. She moved in close, really close, and threw her arms up in the air, writhing suggestively. Over the music, Adam bellowed,

"When did Shakira get here, and what'd you do with Jacey?"

She laughed and kept on dancing, really getting into it now. An entire bottle of Patron Tequila ended up in her hands as if by magic. Like a pro, she tipped her head back, poured a mouthful, passed it to Adam.

"You wanna see Shakira?" she asked playfully, imitating the star's hip bounces, belly rolls, and shoulder shimmies. It felt so liberating! The music had gotten more intense, and partiers poured onto the floor, bopping to Beyoncé's "Irreplaceable," singing, *"To the left, to the left,"* and then to Rhianna's "SOS," and then, in homage to the designer, to Gwen Stefani's "Rich Girl."

That one nearly stopped Jacey in her dance tracks. Last time Jacey'd heard that song, she had felt as if had been written just for her. 'Cause at that moment, she really did have *"all the riches in the world, baby."* She'd been in a secluded cove, with Matt. She saw him now, through a slit in the crowd. He was doing shots, and his arm was around some random blond. Jacey moved in his direction, forcing Adam along. The song "Hips Don't Lie" came on when she reached Matt's line of vision.

The dance move she executed would later be tagged a "pelvic earthquake." She pulled up her top so her belly-button was exposed, then did the best, sexiest, most suggestive belly dance ever. As far as anyone could tell, it was all for her dance partner, Adam Pratt.

Two people in the room knew differently.

A crowd had gathered around by the time she finished. They were whistling, hooting, clapping, and stamping their feet. Jacey flushed. And remembered. The last time she'd gotten that kind of reaction from an audience had been when she did *Fall from Grace*. Brought to her courtesy of Matt.

The song changed to "Whenever, Wherever," another hip-swiveler. The swivels came more and more naturally every time the bottle was passed her way. She tucked the bottom of her flowy Stella McCartney top under her bra and shouted, "I'm *ab-tastic*! I just made up a word!"

She was so in the moment! So in the groove, feeling nothing but the music and her own sweaty, feverish body. Adam was into it, too, and they hip-swiveled together, grinding and bumping. She held him tight during a John Mayer song, then fell against him and let her fingers play his spine like a saxophone.

Soon, however, Ivy and Dash were in her face, saying something about toning it down, and "that's enough for now." Jacey waved them away and kept dancing. She got a great idea when she accidentally bumped into a coffee table. Jacey hopped onto it—playing to the crowd now.

Someone had put a bottle in her hand again, which she sang into as if it were a microphone, while shaking her booty. The crowd was with her, egging her on. All at once, someone else was on the table.

Kate Summers had joined her! Oh, Kate! Jacey *lo-o-o-oved* Kate! And whoever said they were rivals, well, pooh on them! She slipped her arm around Katie's waist, and the two sang along with the music, warbling loudly, and badly, to OutKast's classic "Hey Ya."

Jacey snuck a sly peek at Matt. She'd gotten his attention now. He looked flabbergasted, and not in a good way. He made no move to remove Buxom Girl's hand from his thigh.

"Adam!" Jacey called. "C'mon up, we'll dance a three-way! Whoo-*hoo*! Jacey was shocked—shocked!—that Adam didn't jump up. What was wrong with him? Oh, well, whatever. She and Kate could kick this by themselves.

"Jacey," Kate called, "I jus' wantcha ta know it wassn' my . . . *hiccup!* . . . idea."

"I know," giggled Jacey. "I got up here first."

"Not the coffee table, the Teen Choice thingy. They made it look like I said you shouldn't . . . *hic* . . . be legible."

Jacey wasn't sure what Kate meant, but she decided to forgive her anyway. Into her line of vision came Ivy,

Emilio, Dash, Aja, Desi, Mike, even the evil Kia, all trying to cajole—she loved that word ca-*JO*-eL!—her to come down. They were so sweet. Jacey loved her posse; and maybe Kia wasn't such a chowderhead. Maybe that was just her image! Jacey cracked herself up at that, since Kia worked for Cinnamon, whose motto was: *Image Is Everything.* She blew kisses at them, but refused to descend. "This is too much fun! You guys should get up here!"

"Body shots!" Someone yelled. "Let's do body shots!"

"What're body shots?" she shouted to Kate.

"You lay down on the table, and they lick tequila from your belly button!" Kate pulled her top up to demonstrate. She tried to pour the contents of Jacey's bottle into her belly button, but it dripped down to her knees. Which puzzled them both.

"Cool! Let's do it!" Jacey cried.

That was when Sierra intervened. Or tried to. And then Adam. And Desi and Mike and the whole pissy posse. It seemed as if the arms of a centipede were reaching for Jacey and Kate, trying to pull them off the table.

The starlets had the same thought at the same instant.

"Thelma and Louise!" they shouted as they flew off the table—right into the hot tub. The bubbly water splashed! Oooh, it was warm, *delicioso,* and wet! It didn't taste that good, though. Who knew? When she broke the surface, her beautiful top had flown back, covering her face. Uh-oh, Jacey realized, she'd gotten her designer duds—or was it dud?—all soaked. "Wet T-shirt contest!" she yelled, pulling it tight over her chest, sticking her tatas out.

"*Stell-a!*" Her father used to howl that. She couldn't remember why. So she howled, too: "*Stell-a!* Will it shrink?"

The last thing she remembered before everything went black was Adam's powder blue shirtsleeve and Mike's waterproof watch. The boys seemed to latch on to her, and then they were tugging her out of the Jacuzzi as she kicked happily at the water. That was what got tattooed on her brain. Also, the look on Matt's face as he passed her on his way out. She couldn't form the thought just then, but later she would. He was disgusted.

jaceyfan blog

Jacey's Vegas Hot Mess of the Week— See Her on YouTube!

Jacey, we hardly knew ye. You've made mistakes, hit some speed bumps, done the diva thing, but girl, this time you hit the jackpot of shame! You acted like a wasted slut in front of a room full of VIPs— Paris and her ilk would be so proud. Are you doing drugs? Is this what booze does to you? Or have we finally witnessed the real you, without your battalion of agents and advisers to protect your good-girl image?

Or, is it possible you didn't *know* that everything that happens in Vegas ends up on streaming video? And comes with consequences? Like, let me be the first to announce: you got fired from that high-profile, megabucks iPod gig. Megacorporations, even the cool ones, no likey sexy, sauced-up underage bad girls.

What next? We predict: remorse, redemption, and rehab.

Speaking of a primo candidate for rehab, Matt

Canseco busted out his bad-boy moves in Vegas. After Jacey's scene-stealing table dance and hot-tub dunk, Canseco hit the casino. Hard. Got into a brawl at the poker table. Chairs were hurled, chips flung, punches thrown! Security guards escorted him to his room—where the raucous party continued. Sources say Matt was joined by his posse, and a parade of sweet, nubile young things. The party escalated, and damages for at least one pricey hotel suite will come out of his next paycheck!

Matt left the next day on the arm of a mystery brunette, a real stunner.

But here's the best part. Jacey doesn't care. She's clearly moved on. Putting the moves on Adam Pratt like that? Lovebirds, get a room next time.

Chapter Fourteen

Jacey's Achy, Breaky Hangover

Jacey's first hangover was supersized. It came with dizziness, nausea, vomiting, a pounding headache, and a whopping topping of shame and embarrassment.

She'd completely and totally humiliated herself with her booze-infused PDI (public display of idiocy). She'd ignored her friends, used Adam like a tool, and ruined a priceless, one-of-a-kind ensemble, right in front of the designer, no less! At a VIP-only party deemed so elite that wishful wannabes lined the street to get in. She'd sashayed past them like royalty, only to act like a drunken jester, an obnoxious, oversexed, party girl, later on. She'd trashed her image and torched her self-esteem. All over a guy who was over her.

Not her finest moment.

Her friends had sprung into action, rushed her back to Malibu, tucked her in, drawn the shades, and placed a bucket by the side of the bed . . . just in case.

It wasn't until well into the following day that the room stopped spinning, the aspirins kicked in, and the green tea and dry toast actually stayed down. Before she left her room to face her friends, she called Cinnamon.

For the first time ever, she couldn't get through.

Kia, acting as Cinnamon's gatekeeper, informed Jacey that the agent was too busy doing damage control to come to the phone. Jacey swallowed the instinct to growl, "Who are *you* to keep me from speaking to her?" Good thing, too, because the next thing Kia said—with what surely sounded like a smirk—stunned her into silence.

"You lost the iPod deal."

The blogger had already guessed that, but the reality horrified her way more than the rumor.

Jacey composed a long, hyperapologetic e-mail that she sent to Cinnamon and the iPod reps. She took responsibility for everything that'd she'd done and offered to make up for it in any way she could.

Then she called Adam. He picked up on the first ring.

"Jacey! Or is it Shakira?" he cracked. "How're you feeling the day after?"

"Crappy. Regretful," she admitted, surprised at his light tone. "I acted like the biggest jerk in the world. I'm so, so sorry."

"Sorry for what? You were a *pisser*!" Adam chuckled. "That party was the most fun I've had in, oh, hours!"

"I'm sure I was great entertainment," she conceded, "but I called to apologize—"

Adam cut her off. "For what, pretending you were into me in a pathetic attempt to make Canseco jealous?"

"You . . . you knew?" Jacey's stomach sank.

"I'm superficial, Jacey, not stupid."

"You weren't hurt?" she asked meekly.

"Hurt? More like, helped. Those pictures ended up in the tabs, on YouTube, and I was in them! My name's getting out there," he said proudly. "Jacey Chandliss, you officially have a season pass to use me whenever you want—especially when there's a photog around."

Good old Adam, the one person you could count on to stay true to himself.

She found her friends splayed out on the front porch, sunbathing. Dash had slathered his pale skin with globs of sunscreen. Ivy had a silver reflector tucked under her chin, and Desi was in the fetal position, snoring. Jacey came up behind Dash and smoothed out the sunscreen on his back and shoulders.

"America's next top screw-up is awake," she announced. "Thanks for taking care of me, guys."

"Don't be so hard on yourself," Dash said, propping himself up on his elbows. "All you did was make a complete and utter fool of yourself—"

"Guilty as charged," Jacey moaned.

"So you got wasted, drunk, and disorderly," Dash continued, as if it was no big deal. "At least you didn't go all Michael Richards and hurl racial insults, or Naomi Campbell and hurl cell phones." He chuckled. "The only person who got hurt was you."

"And my career," she said glumly. "I'm guessing there won't be any superhero parts in my future."

"Get over it, get over yourself." This from Ivy, who remained motionless, her eyes closed and her sun reflector in place. "You lost the iPod deal is all."

"Wait a minute. What don't I know?" Jacey asked suspiciously. "You're both awfully calm and forgiving about this."

"This is Hollywood, not Bloomfield Hills," Ivy yawned. "You're headline news now—until you get overshadowed by the next surprise scandal. And how long do you think that will take?"

"My own agent won't even speak to me."

"And yet, she just called me." Ivy let the sun reflector fall onto her taut abs and turned her head in Jacey's direction.

"What'd Cinnamon say?" Jacey asked tentatively.

"You are damned lucky to have her—and Peyton—on your team. They called an emergency five a.m. damage-control meeting to decide how to handle this."

"They did?"

"Oh, grow up, doe-eyes," Ivy snapped. "If you don't know them by now, you don't deserve them."

Jacey flushed, stung.

"Sorry." Ivy was quick to apologize. "It's sleep-deprivation. It feels like I've been up for days. And I drank too much in Vegas, too. And sometimes I get frustrated by your naïveté. Cinnamon and Peyton work around the clock for you. That's what power agents and pricey publicists do."

"Are they freaked about the iPod thing?" Jacey asked.

"They're over it," Ivy said. "They've got bigger problems. Like plugging the dam. They can't deny what happened, so they're spinning the circumstances."

"What are they going to say? Exhaustion?" Desi, awake now, guessed. "Dehydration? That's what they always say when a star has partied too hard."

"Too played," Ivy replied. "Even the public knows what that really means."

"Temporary insanity?" Dash ventured.

"Close," Ivy said. "They've leaked a story to the press that Jacey's drink was spiked with some kind of drug. Either amphetamines or Ecstasy. And since Jacey hardly drinks, the combination caused a bizarre allergic reaction; she just went manic."

"That's genius!" Desi exclaimed admiringly.

Ivy smiled softly. "That was mine. I thought of it."

I should be grateful, Jacey thought. If anyone actually believes that excuse, no one will ever know why I made such a spectacle of myself—the really humiliating part. Except for Matt and Adam, she thought. They knew.

"But who would spike her drink?" Dash tried to follow the logic of the lie.

"We're hinting that it could've been someone who had something to gain," Ivy said with a sly smile.

Kate. Or her people, on her behalf. Kate was also culpable in the incident, but she didn't have a precious image to maintain. She hadn't come from the heartland, been America's choice for *Generation Next*.

Jacey went back into the house, feeling worse than ever. Boneheaded Adam was thrilled, and her agent and cousin had constructed a web of lies, implicating an innocent—albeit also drunk—person. And Desi thought it was genius!

What was she doing here?

Jacey had never needed a reality check more. She called home. In a lengthy, late afternoon phone call, Jacey told her parents everything and warned them not to believe the drug story her people were planting.

That was when Cece Chandliss Taylor said something that allowed Jacey to forgive herself.

"You've lost perspective, honey. You're seventeen years old," her mom said. "Can anyone even count the number of kids your age who get drunk and do things they regret? They get phony IDs off the Internet—I hear that's easy. Some of the kids go bar-hopping, even picking up strangers. Some of them get behind the wheel and hurt other people, or worse. I can't tell you how many stories I've heard. Nothing you did comes close!

"Am I happy you got drunk? Am I condoning your behavior? Of course not. But to put it in perspective, you were at a private party, surrounded by your friends. You weren't driving, you weren't angry, you didn't insult anyone, and no one got hurt.

"As your stepfather reminded me, if you weren't a target for those horrible tabloids and that vicious blog, no one aside from your parents would care. No one would know! And," she added, "I know there's a lesson in this, Jacey. You'll figure it out. We have faith in you, sweetheart."

The tears were flowing like a river as Jacey thanked her mom. The sick feeling in her stomach dissipated.

In the end, Ivy had nailed it. Who knew if anyone believed their fake excuse, but after a couple of days, Jacey's Vegas antics landed in the "so five minutes ago" column. She'd been upstaged by a trio of other misbehaving Hollywood stars' transgressions: a DUI, an outing, an unplanned pregnancy.

As Jacey's mom had reminded her, what she'd done hadn't come close to those things. And there was even a bonus: instead of making Matt jealous, she'd turned him off completely, and proved she was too young to handle her liquor—or her disappointment. She wouldn't be hearing from, or caring about, Matt Canseco anytime soon.

Call it her silver lining.

Parents Threaten Rehab!

Uh-oh, looks like Jacey's gone and crossed the line—all the way back to Michigan. I can report that the folks in Bloomfield Hills are not happy with their underage daughter's recent booze-infused dance and dive antics. They're embarrassed, humiliated, and, from what I hear, on the phone with rehab facilities. Check it: since Jacey's only seventeen, Mom and Pop Chandliss are within their legal rights to send her away for intensive counseling. If they do, will she get out in time for the Teen Choice Awards? Or will her shakin' shenanigans render her MIA on the big day? And how will newest flame, Adam Pratt, feel about that? It was her boyfriend, you remember, who pulled her out of the hot tub that night—can he get her out of the hot seat now?

Oh, and by the way, that flimsy cover-up Jacey's people tried to sell, that "someone" spiked her drink? Yeah, right. Next time, go with exhaustion or dehydration.

Chapter Fifteen

Primping, Pampering, and Power-Shopping

The following week was dedicated to the Teen Choice Awards. Preparation went into overdrive. Translation: shopping; pampering; getting styled, made-up, and deluged with freebies. In other words, the whole showbiz standard for awards-show nominees; even those who, like Jacey, had misbehaved.

Cinnamon and Peyton kicked things off by hosting a girls-only party at the trendiest hand-and-foot spa in town. Jacey had never heard of L.A. Vie L'Orange, but the moment she entered the lush, cozy salon, she put their number on speed dial. It was manicure/pedicure heaven.

L.A. Vie L'Orange specialized in extreme pampering. Jacey, Desi, Ivy, Cinnamon, and Peyton were the pamperees. The vibe was serene; the decor, earthy, warm, and woodsy; and the aroma the sweet scent of orange-vanilla candles. Tall, thronelike wicker and cushioned cabanas were arranged in a semicircle. Each had a foot-soaking tub and a private manicure table.

"Oh, my God, I love it here!" Ivy's eyes danced. "I'm making weekly appointments."

When Desi scooted into her cabana, her tootsies didn't even touch the tiled floor. She looked like the classic Lily Tomlin character, Edith Ann, a wee girl dwarfed by an oversize chair, but that didn't dim her awe—or her nose for nearby sweets. "I smell chocolate-chip cookies!" she squealed, her eyes wide.

Peyton had ordered a tray of the fresh-baked goodies to munch on. "We'll do more nibbles later," the publicist promised, "but I had to see who I could tempt with these first. They are to die for." Everyone except ever-vigilant Cinnamon was led into temptation. In Desi's case, twice.

The group scanned the menu of treatments. The spa offered every kind of foot-soothing pedicure and exfoliating manicure, including one specifically designed for "waving at fans in the bleachers" and "holding a golden statuette."

"That's the one you're getting, Jacey," Desi decreed, "'cause you are so gonna win."

"She gets a surfboard if she wins," Ivy said. "We should think about matching her nail polish to the dominant color on the board."

"Excellent idea!" Cinnamon agreed, excitedly adding, "Then we'll get the dress and shoes to match the nails. I like it, Ivy."

Jacey sank into her chaise, too relaxed to comment on the "bass-ackwards" (as Dash would say) logic. She snuck a peek at Cinnamon. Jacey hadn't discussed "the incident in Las Vegas" with either her agent or her publicist. But as Ivy assured her, they did seem over it. Peyton had hired a photographer to snap "candids" of Jacey getting ready for the big event. They hoped the photos would appear in *People* magazine.

During the next few delicious hours, the group fully hydrated their hands, submitted to seaweed oatmeal scrubs, grape-seed-oil and hot-paraffin wraps, and, finally, foot massages with Dead Sea salt and stones.

More food was delivered, and they noshed, nibbled, and talked. Tensions faded; it was girlfriend time. Until Cinnamon remarked, "In all the excitement and hubbub, we never addressed *Generation Next* being up for Choice Reality Show."

There's a question here somewhere, Jacey thought warily, watching the manicurist shape her nails.

"If *Gen Next* wins, do they want Jacey to accept?" asked Desi.

"Half credit. In the event of a win, the producers have asked for Jacey *and* Carlin—Kia tells me she's stayed in town to work on her stand-up routine—to accept on behalf of the show.

"And," Cinnamon said quickly, before the girls could object, "the Slickity Jeans people would also like that."

Protests erupted from her posse, but Jacey quickly agreed to the plan. Partly because she felt morally obligated to support the reality show that had put her on the map. But mostly, bucking Cinnamon was not a thing she wanted to do right now. She was an actress, she told herself; surely she could act as if she and Carlin were cool.

"As long as we don't have to sit near her skankness," Ivy huffed.

"Speaking of who sits where," Cinnamon said, segueing to the next topic, "Jacey will be in the front row, so she can easily get on-and offstage while she's presenting and, hopefully, accepting."

"Where are we sitting?" Desi asked.

Peyton fielded that one. "One of you—or Jacey's date—will sit on her left. Cinnamon will be on her right. Everyone else, including myself, has assigned seats in the balcony, with celebrity relatives, entourages, and fans."

Desi scrunched up her pert nose; she was definitely not pleased with that arrangement.

"Wait, what about Kate?" Ivy suddenly asked.

"Behind Jacey. The *Four Sisters* team is grouped together," Peyton replied.

The mention of Kate set off a wave of gossip. Desi had read that she was planning to wear a killer Zac Posen dress with a plunging neckline. Ivy heard that Kate had snagged next season's most coveted electric blue, peep-toe satin pumps with jeweled heels from Prada. And then there was the buzz that never went away: Kate's people had somehow rigged the vote.

"What could they have done, spiked my drink so I'd act like a buffoon?" Jacey meant that to come out as a joke. It didn't.

"What could they *do*?" echoed Cinnamon. "Anything from bribing voters to hacking into computers and changing the outcome. And everything in between."

Jacey refused to believe that Kate would hang with cheaters. She hadn't suddenly become Kate's BFF, their recent drunken duet aside—she just wanted to trust that you won, or lost, the Teen Choice Awards fair and square. Her idealism about fair play in Hollywood had evaporated months ago, but some things had to be real, right? If she did win, as most were still predicting, it would be because enough fans had voted for her—just like what happened on *Generation Next*.

Sipping champagne, Peyton casually asked, "Have you decided whom you'll be bringing?"

Jacey shook her head. Not surprisingly, Adam Pratt had volunteered. Multiple times. Jacey refused to add fuel to the fire of their oh-so-faux romance. She'd politely turned him down.

Once upon a time, way before Carlin hit the sand with Matt, before Las Vegas, where she'd stuck a kitchen knife in her chances with him, Jacey had dreamed about asking him. As a friend.

Now? Not so much.

Even though Matt Canseco detested the pomp, paparazzi, and phoniness of red carpet "circuses," as he called them, Jacey had used to think he'd do it for her. And here was the kicker: Matt was actually coming to the Teen Choice Awards this year. A movie he'd filmed in the spring was up for Choice Chase Scene. Matt would be there to support his costars, and would, no doubt, stay far away from her.

"You know," Cinnamon put in, "if you want to go with a celebrity, any of the hot guys my firm represents would jump at the chance to escort you."

★ ★ ★

Jacey still hadn't decided who'd be on her arm later that week, when Team Jacey started power-shopping for shoes and accessories, trying on various shades of makeup, and spending hours at the hairdresser, fiddling with updos, extensions, bangs, full-out curly, slick and straight, or naturally wavy, with or without highlights.

At least this was one event where she didn't have to obsess about the perfect dress. If she believed the tabloids, everything she'd worn before had been a disaster.

Criticizing stars' outfits used to be entertaining when she and her friends did it, but it wasn't so great when you were the one being picked apart.

The look at the Teen Choice Awards was casual, funky, and fun.

Translation: she'd wear Slickity Jeans. And a hip top that went with her raspberry nail polish—and with the surfboard award, should she get one—without seeming too "matchy-matchy."

Jacey chose buckled knee-high Dolce & Gabbana boots and an excellent sparkly red spaghetti-strap top with drapey cap sleeves. Her hairstyle would be loose and soft around the face, with low, cascading waves; her makeup would be subtle; the only jewelry she'd wear was a bunch of ropey, cause-related bracelets and an angel-wing necklace.

A spray-on tan, lip gloss, a cool bag, and she was essentially good to go.

Except, that is, for a date.

And a speech.

Those missing links got filled in the night before the show, when Jacey found herself alone in the beach house with Desi. Ivy had a "thing" with Emilio, and Dash and Aja were off to catch a concert by the Bravery.

"Where's Mike tonight?" Jacey asked, idly flipping through the latest copy of *Malibu Magazine*.

"He had something to deal with," said Desi, who was on her knees in front of the big-screen TV, futzing with the remote. She was a terrible liar.

"No one wanted me to be alone on the night before the awards. So you got stuck babysitting," Jacey deduced.

"No way!" Desi protested, never taking her eyes off the TV. "I need to TiVo a bunch of stuff."

"Right, I'll just bet." Jacey shook her head. "What am I gonna do with you guys?" Impulsively, she scooted down onto the floor next to Des and hugged her. A better question would have been, what would she do without them.

"Seriously, Des," she said, "call Mike. I'm fine. I promise not to do anything stupid, like get drunk or send a sobby e-mail to Matt. I'll just watch a DVD and work on my speech. How's that?"

"I can help with the speech—or you can try it out on me. How's *that*?" Desi wasn't going to budge.

Secretly, Jacey was relieved. Being alone could lead to brooding. And in all truthiness—her new favorite word— she didn't have other friends she could call. Everyone she knew either worked for her, was in Matt's posse, or were rivals, like Kate and Sierra. Adam was not an option, espe- cially if she wasn't walking the red carpet with him. Which she wasn't. "So, should we go out to eat, or call in?" she asked.

Desi sprang to her feet, darted into the kitchen, and returned with a fistful of take-out menus.

Jacey chuckled, "Did they tell you to keep me hostage inside—and out of trouble?"

"Something like that," Desi conceded. "Anyway, tomorrow's a big day. You should chill tonight."

Later, over sushi, sashimi, and garlic noodles from Nobu, Jacey mused, "What a year it's been, huh, Des? Totally yo-yo—pinch-me highs and stinky lows."

"If you wanted to quit—to go back to Michigan—that would be okay. We'd all understand and support you. I would go back with you."

Jacey gave her a look. I wouldn't ask you to, she

thought. You've got Mike, Ivy's hoping for a career, and Dash has college classes and a great guy out here. And me? *My* constant companions are publicity-hound Adam and the blogger!

As if reading her mind, Desi blurted out, "I feel bad about the tabloids, Jace. And about your crazy blogger. No one can seem to figure out who it is."

"It's not just the blogger. It's the paparazzi and the tabloids always on my tail. They're so ruthless! What'd I ever do to them to deserve these attacks on me?" She griped.

"They're jealous," Desi said sagely.

"I always thought it would feel good to be envied. I was wrong. It's rotten." Jacey's voice broke, and she stifled a sniffle.

"You hardly ever show us if you're upset," Desi said. "You can, you know."

"If you let it get to you, you're just making a bigger deal of whatever lies they're spreading. Or . . ." Jacey said, "we're spreading."

"Probably the Matt thing is harder than the blogger, anyway," Desi reflected. "But you'll get over it. There's a million guys who'd kill to go out with you."

"A million, huh?" Jacey only wanted one. One in a million—who didn't want anything from her, had nothing to gain by hanging with her, and just wanted to be with her. A guy who'd wipe hamburger drippings off her chin.

"Being a star gets you a lot of stuff. But it doesn't protect you from heartbreak," Desi said.

Jacey began to laugh. It just sounded so . . . clichéd. And ridiculous. And . . . heartfelt. It sounded like her best friend in the world talking. She'd work on her "just in case I win" speech later. But one thing was decided. She knew who her date would be.

Who Should She Go Out With? Vote!

While everyone's debating Jacey's chances of winning—or losing—the Teen Choice Awards, here's another debate—one you can join!

Which guy is she into? Is she still pining for Matt Canseco? What're the odds that she's forgiven—or forgotten—Matt's cheating on her with Carlin?

Is her thing with Adam Pratt the real deal? (Sure looked that way!)

Or, is she using young Adam in a pathetic bid to win Matt back? (Another interpretation!)

Who do *you* think she belongs with? Text your votes to me, your friendly anonymous blogger, and I'll put 'em up on my site.

But wait—before you vote, you do want to remember that Matt left Las Vegas with a long-legged stunner. A mystery brunette he seemed awfully close to. Don't believe *me*, check the tabloids!

Chapter Sixteen

The Teen Choice Awards!

Sparkly, high-spirited, and "groovescent"—that was how Jacey summed up the vibe outside the Teen Choice Awards. The event was held at the Gibson Amphitheatre at Universal Studios CityWalk, an outdoor venue normally crammed with wide-eyed tourists. Tonight, there were hordes of hyperexcited, fans gathered behind the roped-off red carpet wielding cameras, handmade posters, and autograph books.

Their excitement was contagious, thought Jacey as her delighted date, Desi, guided her into the crowd. She wanted to oblige as many fans as possible with hugs, handshakes, autographs, and snapshots. For the first time since being nominated, it hit her: this was why she did it.

This was why she was an actress. Fulfilling oneself went only so far in showbiz. Without an audience to appreciate your work, you didn't get famous, and you didn't get a chance at the parts you wanted.

She reached out to sign a poster that read, *"We Love You, Jacey!"* She loved them—she owed them!—right back.

The red carpet hosted everyone who was anyone with teen appeal: Gwen Stefani, Pete Wentz, Alicia Keys, and Kelly Clarkson represented the music-heads; movie stars like Cameron Diaz, Ashton Kutcher, Julia Barton, Johnny Depp, and Keira Knightley were out in force. Jacey waved to Kate Summers, who looked a little stunned, being led around by her agent and trailed by Sierra Tucson.

TV stars from the casts of *Grey's Anatomy*, *High School Musical*, *Heroes*, and *Ugly Betty* elicited the loudest screams. The most pointing and jumping up and down was for the reality-show stars, like Tyra Banks and some of the other top models; Simon Cowell and Paula Abdul from *American Idol*; and, of course, the *Dancing with the Stars* favorites.

The stars air-kissed, high-fived, and gushed over one another, while trying, and mostly succeeding—thanks to highly paid stylists and hairdressers—to look as if they hadn't put any effort into looking great.

The press shoved microphones into famous faces, and

photographers snapped away without pausing. All under the megabrightest klieg lights Jacey had ever seen.

Jacey had been right to go glitzy-casual. The jeans, the top, the boots—it all worked, fit right in with her red-carpet peers. Some of the guys, like Chad Michael Murray and Justin Timberlake, wore jeans and T-shirts; girls wore everything from tank tops and tight tops to flirty sun-dresses and microminis. Desi looked adorable in her breezy Luca Luca dress.

Carlin, having appointed herself the official ambassa-dor for *Generation Next*, sought Jacey out. She was accompanied by her shadow, housemate, and now BFF, Kia. It was hard to decide which of them was the bigger fashion disaster. Kia wore thick Goth eyeliner, her trade-mark scraggly black hairdo, black leggings, a black turtle-neck, and various-skull-and-crossbones pendants. How could Cinnamon have allowed it, Jacey wondered? Carlin had chosen microshorts and a plunging V-neck top embroidered with huge gold sequins. Fringes all around the bottom made it worse.

Oy, as Dash would have said. It was too much and too little at the same time. Dash, Ivy, Cinnamon, and Peyton were a few paces behind Jacey and Desi, ready to steer them toward the awaiting press corps and help out should they need rescuing.

In light of recent events, that seemed inevitable.

"Tell us what really went down in Vegas? Do you think Kate spiked your drink?" A reporter zoomed in, without so much as a hello or even a "Who are you wearing?"

"There's no evidence of that," said Jacey, putting on her best perplexed face.

"Who else would do that? Who has a grudge against you?" Another nosy newsman put in.

"I have no idea," Jacey said brightly. "Maybe it's the person behind the Jacey blog."

"Good answer!" Desi whispered, patting her on the back.

"Do you think you'll win tonight?" asked the friendlier reporter from *Access Hollywood*.

"I hope so! But there are four wonderful breakout actresses in my category, so who knows?"

The gossip reporter from the E! cable channel wanted to know if she'd seen Matt Canseco yet.

Jacey's stomach lurched, but she hid it well. "No, I haven't," was her brief response, before Peyton pulled her off to the next interview, and then, thankfully, inside.

Once inside the theater, safely ensconced between Desi and Cinnamon, Jacey greeted her *Four Sisters* costars warmly—including Kate and Sierra. She waved to Adam, who was seated on an aisle several rows back, and tried to pick out Ivy, Dash, and Peyton way up in the balcony, while trying to convince herself she wasn't scanning the audience for Matt.

Just before the live show started its broadcast, someone tapped her on the shoulder, and a slim hand offered a flask filled with liquor. Jacey quickly shook her head no before Cinnamon could see anything. There would be more than a few looped presenters, performers, and winners up on that stage, she thought, before noticing Kate, taking a long slug behind her.

"Are you excited?" Cinnamon asked, leaning over and squeezing her hand.

She was, actually. It didn't take long before Jacey got caught up in the show, nearly forgetting she wasn't just a guest there. The host was the zany comedian Jack Black, and he was hysterical! Jacey rocked out to performances by Fergie and Fall Out Boy and found herself cheering for such winners as the latest Harry Potter, for Choice Movie; *Heroes,* for Choice TV Show, and of course, Dr. McDreamy and Meredith, for Choice Lip Lock.

At the commercial break, she and Adam were escorted backstage—it'd soon be their turn to present the award for Choice Reality Show. If *Generation Next* won, she'd already be onstage, and Carlin could smoothly join her. No doubt Carlin already had her speech prepared, thought Jacey.

Backstage, dozens of crew members ran around with walkie-talkies and scripts. A wall lined with surfboards was close to the stage.

An assistant handed Adam and Jacey their scripts—the lines they were supposed to say while presenting—although the two had already studied them. Besides that, their dialogue would be up on the teleprompter while they were onstage, just in case panic set in.

"You guys are in the Suite B dressing room," another assistant, consulting a clipboard, told them. "We've got thirteen dressing rooms here," he boasted, as he accompanied them down the hallway. "You've got one of the coolest."

"One of?" Adam kidded. "What are the others?"

"The Headliner Suite rules. It's tricked out with couches, chairs, a fully stocked bar, even a piano! It's right across the hall from yours."

"Maybe we'll check it out," Adam said to Jacey.

"Okay, guys," the assistant told them, "you've got fifteen minutes. Rehearse, relax, make yourselves comfortable. There's a TV in the corner, so you can monitor what's happening onstage. Someone will come get you when it's your turn."

Their dressing room had comfy leather chairs; tables laden with trays of sandwiches; a bar stocked with water, iced tea, and soft drinks; and a private bathroom. Jacey settled into one of the club chairs and went over the script.

Adam was pacing the room, studying his script. This was probably his first time in front of a live audience, Jacey realized, with a jolt of tenderness.

"You nervous?" Jacey asked, looking over at him. He looked good tonight, she admitted to herself. He was wearing a denim shirt to offset his baby blue eyes, and his hair was just the right amount of tousled. He'd be a good catch for someone, she thought, if he could dredge up some real self-esteem and realize he didn't need to attach himself to a bigger star to gain popularity.

"Yeah," he admitted ruefully, running his fingers through his hair. "Kind of."

"Chill, it'll be fine. Let's rehearse. If you panic—which you won't, I'll have your back."

Adam perched on the wide leather arm of her chair. "You look amazing tonight, Jacey."

"Right back atcha," she smiled.

Adam's arm was now resting across the back of her chair. "I really like you."

"Correction. You really like being photographed with me."

"No," he said quietly, "it's more than that. There's a

connection between us. You can't deny it."

Jacey squirmed. What was he doing?

"Come on, admit it. We spend a lot of time together, and I can tell you enjoy it. You're into me, too."

"Not like that, Adam," she said gently. "In Las Vegas, you said you understood. I'm really sorry if I led you to believe otherwise."

"You say you weren't into me, but your body language said you were." He actually sounded confident now.

"Adam, I was so drunk that night. You can't—"

"In vino veritas," he said, mispronouncing it as *ve-REE-taz*.

"*VE*-ri-tas," she corrected him. It was Latin, and it meant that, under the influence of wine, people say what they really feel—things they'd never dare say when sober; the truth comes out when drinking wine or, in Jacey's case, tequila.

"Adam." Jacey stared at him meaningfully.

"I know you're not over Matt. I can wait." He was serious.

"This isn't the time, or the place. . . ."

He leaned over to envelop her in his arms and kiss her. She jumped up so fast he lost his balance and fell sideways into the empty chair.

Breezily, she said, "I'm going to check out the

Headliner Suite—be back in a minute."

That was a bad idea.

Matt Canseco was there, hanging with Jack Black, Drew Barrymore, and a few other real-deal A-list stars. They barely blinked when she busted in, uninvited.

Matt, however, inhaled sharply. He hadn't expected to see her, and he stared openly.

Jacey's heart raced. She wanted to say, "Sorry, wrong room," but she couldn't breathe, let alone speak. She tried to back out the door, but Matt called out, "Wait—hold up!" The next thing she knew, his hand was wrapped around her arm. Jacey froze in her tracks.

Her brain buzzed, while her legs turned to jelly. *Please let go! Please let go!* She'd be called on to the stage at any minute. She couldn't let Adam go on by himself!

"Can we talk, just for a sec?" Matt asked gently, guiding her into the hallway.

"I don't have time, I have to go—" She looked around for an escape.

"You look beautiful, Jacey," he said softly, grazing her arm with his knuckles.

As always, Matt got her motor racing. The thick, shaggy hair, the penetrating eyes, the charcoal lashes, the smooth planes of his sharp cheekbones, begging to be caressed.

"We should talk," he said carefully, still stroking her arm, "after the show."

Fury and longing squished her heart. Jacey forced herself to look away. How he could look so gorgeous and be so tender, so complimentary? How could he have hooked up with Carlin? And some Las Vegas mystery brunette? How could he continue to toy with her, but never choose her?

No, she didn't want to—couldn't bear to—talk to him.

"Jacey! They're calling us!" Adam flew over.

Matt cupped her chin, forcing her to look at him. "Have fun out there, Dimples. . . . I hope you win," he whispered.

Adam swept her toward the stage, where they were just being introduced.

"Our next presenters are the stars of the upcoming blockbuster *Galaxy Rangers*. She's a *Generation Next* winner and nominee tonight; he's her costar, and a fast-rising up-and-comer himself! Give it up for Jacey Chandliss and Adam Pratt!"

The audience broke into spirited applause. Jacey knew without looking that Dash, Ivy, and Desi were on their feet, clapping wildly and whistling.

And just like that—snap!—Jacey turned it on.

Beaming, pointing at Desi, waving to the fans in the balcony, Jacey was luminous onstage. When the cheering died down, Jacey read her first line. "How cool is this, Adam, being here at the Teen Choice Awards?"

"It's amazing!" he exclaimed. "But I'm a little disappointed."

Jacey's eyebrows went up. What the—? He's going off script already?

"I kind of hoped we'd get to present Choice Lip Lock," Adam said smoothly, as if those words had been on the teleprompter. Which they were not.

Jacey had no choice. She went with it. "Why is that, Adam?"

"Well, we *do* have a love scene in *Galaxy Rangers*. I'm thinking we could be nominated next year."

"Maybe you and your mirror," she one-upped him jauntily, fuming inside. The audience roared.

Adam didn't get flustered. "Good one, Jacey! Maybe we should read the nominees."

"For Choice Reality Show, the nominees are . . ." As practiced, they took turns reading the list: *The Amazing Race*; *American Idol*; *Dancing with the Stars*; *Generation Next*.

"And the surfboard goes to . . ." Adam paused dramatically.

Jacey prayed guiltily: anything but *Generation Next* . . .

". . . *Dancing with the Stars*!" Adam announced. Jacey whooped!

Fan favorites Mario Lopez and Emmitt Smith made their way up to the stage. Someone thrust the surfboard at Jacey. She had just a second to think: Whoa! It's huge. It's bigger than I am. But it does match my nails.

Chapter Seventeen

And the Winner Is . . .

"You were *fabulous* up there," Cinnamon hugged her as Jacey made her way past her agent and back to her seat. "Even when Adam threw you a curveball, with that blatant plug for himself."

"That wasn't the only thing I was unprepared for," Jacey admitted.

"You handled it like a pro," Cinnamon said proudly. "Now comes the real excitement!"

Jacey leaned over and filled Desi in on the encounter with Matt.

"Sorry. I was praying we'd make it through the night without any Matt-sightings," Desi said sympathetically.

"I'm going to run into him—it's inevitable. Might as

well get used to it."

Jacey's mind kept wandering back to Matt as the categories of Choice Grill, Choice Hottie, and Choice Hissy Fit came up. What to do about Adam? What not to do about Matt?

Desi's excitement didn't flag for a minute. She kept turning to Jacey and thanking her, over and over, for the chance to sit right up front, where she could see all the stars and their dates and critique their outfits. Desi kept text-messaging her grandmother and brothers back home.

Choice Breakout Star was still at least twenty minutes away, and Jacey's stomach churned up a storm with each passing moment. Surely, Kate was feeling it, too. Jacey turned around to check on her, only to find her rival and Sierra oblivious, imbibing openly from their stash of tiny liquor bottles. Whatever. Kate probably knew she wasn't going to win. No harm, no foul, in getting smashed.

When the movies nominated for Choice Chase Scene were read, Jacey forced herself to breathe normally. Not that Matt would bound up onstage with the other cast members, but you never knew.

"And the surfboard goes to *Casino Royale!*" Jacey heaved a sigh of relief. An emotional bullet dodged.

If Jacey were keeping score, it would have been 2–0—that is, the results she cared about, Choice Reality

Show and Choice Chase Scene, had gone exactly as she'd hoped. As Choice Breakout grew nearer, she opened her Birkin bag and took out her acceptance speech—which she'd written out on a folded sheet of loose-leaf paper. She went over it again, mentally trying different ways of delivering it. But just as she was about to stash it away, it suddenly hit her—she couldn't go up onstage with the bag. That would look stupid. She stuck the speech in her jeans pocket and went to close her Birkin. That was when she noticed her Razr screen aglow with a text message.

It was from Dash. *U rocked!*

She typed back, *Wait till u hear what happened backstage—drama—x2!*

U can't leave me hanging . . . came the instant response.

Ivy, probably reading over Dash's shoulder, got in on the cyber-convo. *Adam?*

AND Matt, Jacey texted back.

What? What? What? came Ivy's hurried replies.

Adam made a play! M wants 2 talk.

No! No! No! Stay away!

Then Cinnamon caught her texting, and hissed, "Put that away! Your category is right after the commercial! Be ready!"

At the break, some of the audience members got up to

stretch, chat, take calls, and hit the bathroom. Seat fillers were at the ready to take their places temporarily. Fleetingly, Jacey wondered if she had time to go to the ladies' room—and throw up? She never got stage fright, so what was up with the nerves, the dry throat, the perspiration? It couldn't have been about winning. She was prepared, one way or another.

It had to be the backstage boys. Adam, coming on to her—now, of all times! Matt, giving her mixed messages—again! Why did guys always pick the wrong times to do what they thought were the right things?

Jacey focused on mapping out her route up to the stage. She'd have to pass Cinnamon, who was on the aisle. Her agent would most likely be on her feet instantly, ready to give Jacey a half hug and an air kiss. Then, Jacey would flip around and squeeze Desi—or should she squeeze Desi first?

Either way, Cinnamon would back up, leaving her a clear path to the stage. Wait . . . should she run? Trot? Or walk slowly, waving at the fans—and her friends—up in the balcony? But if she was looking up at the balcony, she might not realize where the steps were. She could only imagine what the blog would have to say if she tripped!

Cinnamon nudged her. People were returning to their seats, settling in, and the show was about to get going again. Jacey found herself obsessing about whether to walk slowly and wave or just sprint up the steps to the stage. Or . . . uh-oh, it had just hit her . . . should she kiss and glad-hand people on her way up? She couldn't be so self-absorbed as not to give props to her *Four Sisters* family—and Kate, for sure! Or would that seem like gloating? And why hadn't Cinnamon or Peyton trained her in proper "winning" etiquette?

Well, at least she hadn't forgotten anyone in her prepared speech, she thought confidently. Or had she? She went over the list one more time. That was when she saw a glaring omission. The one person she'd always promised to thank if she ever won a big award—how could she have forgotten? Swiftly, she scribbled, *And to my drama teacher in Bloomfield Hills, my first inspiration, Mrs. . . . Mrs. . . . Ms. . . .* Jacey blanked. How could she forget her name?

Dash would know. She IM'd him and willed him to respond instantly.

Up onstage, the presenters for Choice Breakout were being announced. They were past winners Ashton Kutcher and Jessica Alba. The audience went wild! Jacey started to sweat; her eyes were glued to the cell phone screen. She jumped when Desi grabbed her arm. "Get me an autograph from Ashton, okay?"

"What? Oh . . . sure, Des."

Ashton and Jessica exchanged some scripted patter, reminiscing about their wins in the category. Too soon, they began the list of nominees. Luckily, they described the movies that had kick-started the careers of each nominee.

Still no response from Dash. Maybe he didn't remember? She texted Ivy to tell Dash to look at his messages. The onstage banter was petering out.

Her screen remained frustratingly blank. *C'mon, Dash! I can't forget to thank Mrs. . . . Mrs. . . . What's her name? I know it rhymes with "balloon." Mrs. Prune? Goon?*

"Each of these talented breakouts is bound for A-list fame," they were saying onstage. "But tonight, we can only honor one."

Jacey's stomach Space-Mountained; blood rushed to her ears.

"This year, your choice for female breakout movie star is . . ."

Dash! C'mon, Jacey's head bobbed up and down—checking the stage, checking the tiny glowing screen. A message from Dash! Ye-e-ess!

Mrs. Thune, he'd written. Bless him. Lightning fast, she scrawled it into the blank space in her acceptance speech when she heard the pronouncement: "Kate Summers!"

The audience erupted in thunderous applause. The director, producer, and cast members of *Four Sisters* sprang from their seats, clapping wildly.

"No fair! You were robbed!" Desi shouted. Cinnamon folded in on herself.

Jacey felt as if she'd been kicked in the gut. A sharp pain, then an ache—followed by nausea. *I didn't win? How is that possible? I remembered Mrs. Thune!*

Jacey was reeling, which was why it took her several seconds to realize that expressions of concern, then alarm, and then shock had overtaken the joyful *Four Sisters* celebrants. She whipped her head around.

Kate wasn't there.

"Where is she?" The producer, who had shot down the aisle, nervously demanded of Sierra.

Bleary-eyed Sierra seemed flabbergasted, as if fighting her way out of a fog. "I . . . I . . . don't . . . She was right here!" She looked around wildly.

Onstage, the presenters joked that Kate had chosen the wrong moment to freshen her lip gloss.

"Call her!" hissed the director to a visibly shaking Sierra.

"I'll do it," Jacey offered. Her phone was already out. But Kate's cell went to voice mail after only one ring.

Jacey tried again. And then a third time.

"This wouldn't be happening if you'd won," Desi declared loudly.

The low buzz that had begun in the audience was growing to a dull roar. Jacey heard shocked voices asking, "What's going on?" "Where is she?" "Is this a joke?" "A blooper?"

"This is live TV," the presenters quipped. "No seven-second delays here!"

"Send someone to find her!" barked the producer to the director. "Now!"

Cinnamon came out of her quasi coma; she looked stunned. The stage director signaled for Jessica and Ashton to "stretch" for time.

They ad-libbed, shielding their eyes and pretending to look out over the audience: "Kate, are you hiding?"

"Paging the cast of *Without a Trace*!"

"Maybe she really did 'Break Out'!"

And, "Are we being punk'd?!"

Meanwhile, the mad scramble among the *Four Sisters* reps amped up. The producer finally made an executive decision. "Go up there!" he commanded Sierra. "Accept on her behalf!"

"But I can't!" squealed the panicked actress. "I don't know what to say!"

"Think of something!" The director pleaded. "We need you."

"Say she's dehydrated!" Desi turned to Sierra and snarled. "Or exhausted."

A visibly shaking Sierra, teetering on spike heels, was pushed into the aisle.

Jacey acted on instinct. "Excuse me," she said, crossing in front of Cinnamon. "Sierra! Here—" Jacey pressed her own acceptance speech into the girl's sweaty palm. "Say Kate got called away at the last second—an emergency—but gave you her speech. Start in the middle, with the line that reads, *'And to my Four Sisters* family . . .'"

Cinnamon was aghast. "Why did you do that?"

"I felt sorry for her," Jacey admitted, sliding back into her seat. "She's the only one in the cast who didn't get nominated, and now she's got to accept for someone who did? That's humiliating. Besides, she's half soused and completely panicked. What else could I do?"

Cinnamon leaned forward, cradling her head in her hands.

Desi grumbled, "You should be up there; you should have won—Kate and Sierra owe you, big-time."

Fortified with Jacey's speech, Sierra actually managed to acquit herself well. She probably even convinced some people that Kate had been "suddenly, unexpectedly, called away . . . on a family emergency . . ." and that she had given her the speech she'd written, just in case she won.

Somewhere in Bloomfield Hills, Michigan, Mrs. Thune was racking her brain trying to remember a student named Kate Summers, who was totally indebted to her.

At the final commercial break, the entire audience seemed to be on its collective feet, talking, laughing, and heading to the lobby to make calls. No doubt many were wondering whether the Choice Breakout winner had simply gone MIA, or whether Sierra's excuse was true.

Jacey and Desi started up the aisle, but they didn't get far. The *Four Sisters* team stopped them to thank Jacey profusely for her quick thinking and her help.

They were also stopped by people offering sympathy and/or shock that she hadn't won. But most wanted the scoop on Kate.

Jacey and Desi finally made their way out of the auditorium and into the crowded lobby, where they met up with a bummed-out Ivy and a head-scratching Dash. Both demanded, "Why'd you give Sierra your speech?"

"Trust me, better that Jacey put words *in* her mouth," Desi cracked, "as opposed to what might've come *out* otherwise. Girlfriend was drinking up a storm."

The suggestion of throwing up brought back Jacey's own memory of queasiness. "Think I'll go splash some cold water on my face," she said, gesturing with her thumb toward the ladies' room.

"I say we leave now," Desi decided. "We're all hungry; let's go eat and then hit a club. Jacey can give us the down-low on what happened backstage."

Jacey shook her head. "Leaving now makes me look like a sore loser. There's only two more awards to give out." She headed toward the bathroom.

"Well, we're definitely not going to the afterparty!" huffed Desi.

"We have to," Jacey called back over her shoulder. "If screwing up in Las Vegas cost me the award, it's best to play nice now and do what Cinnamon wants. If she can stand the afterparty, so can we."

The houselights began to flicker, signaling that the show would begin again momentarily. Ivy and Dash headed back to the balcony; Desi called Mike as she waited for Jacey.

The few stragglers left in the bathroom put the finishing touches on their makeup and dried their hands. Jacey gripped the sink and stared into the mirror. Did she look any different from when she'd left the house earlier? Was this the face of a loser? She turned the water on full force to splash her face.

It wasn't until she'd turned the water off and was completely alone in the bathroom that she heard it. At first it sounded like something was vibrating. Or maybe it was more of a purring? Jacey began checking each stall, but all of them were empty. As she advanced down the row, the purring began to sound more like wheezing. It got louder.

The only stall she hadn't checked was the wheelchair-accessible one, which was by itself behind the row of sinks.

Jacey advanced toward it. Yep, the sound was definitely coming from there. So was a reeking odor she couldn't identify; the door was locked.

"Here, kitty, kitty," she called, knocking. "Are you stuck in there?" About to bend over to see if a cat were in there, it hit her. That was not purring—it was snoring! Someone had fallen asleep in the bathroom! The cleaning person, maybe? Only, the odor, stronger as she got closer, was definitely not ammonia.

Eeew. It was *booze,* and it was nauseating. Coughing, Jacey fanned the air around her. Then she crouched down to peer under the stall. A pair of striking electric blue, peep-toe satin pumps with jeweled heels were on the tiled floor. Next season's Pradas. Attached were two sticklike ankles.

"Kate? Kate—are you in there?" She called tentatively. "Are you sick?"

No answer, just more snoring.

Jacey tried again, louder. "Kate, is that you? Do you need help?"

Still no response. Jacey tried to push the door open, but the lock held. A swift kick didn't disengage it, either. Nor did banging on the door and hissing Kate's name. It was time to use brains instead of brawn, she thought.

She'd seen this done on TV shows and in movies, but never in, like, real life.

She pulled her black Amex card out of her bag, slipped it under the lock, and moved it around, all the while whispering Kate's name. She wasn't very good at this.

Before calling Desi in to help her, Jacey gave it one more try. The door swung open, nearly knocking the snoring girl off her perch.

Kate had passed out while sitting up on the closed toilet. Her head was propped against the sink in the stall, and her hair was shooting out in all directions, which would have alarmed her most of all had she been conscious. Kate's bejeweled arms hung limply at her sides; the silver flask lay at her feet.

America's Choice breakout star was as stinking drunk as the proverbial skunk.

"Kate! Kate! Wake up!" Jacey shook the sleeping girl's shoulders.

One eye drifted open, but Kate's makeup had

clumped, dried, and smeared, making it hard for her to separate her lids.

"Jacey?"

It was a total guess; that was how snookered she was.

"Kate, come on, we've got to get out of here," Jacey whispered urgently.

Kate smiled lazily. "Hi, J." She hiccuped, "Wanna sing? I know a song. . . ."

Uh-oh, this sucked worse than anything Jacey might have imagined. How long before others found them? How long before the tabloids and paparazzi would sniff this one out? Missing Winner Found Drunk in Bathroom? What a field day they'd have! Winner Too Hammered to Pick Up an Award Bestowed upon her by Thousands of Impressionable Teens. Kate had messed up big-time. Sierra had participated, too, but it was Kate who'd be eviscerated for it.

Ivy's voice rang in Jacey's head. *What do you care? She deserves it. She stole that award from you.*

And Cinnamon's: *Not your problem. Not your image. Leave her.*

And Desi's: *She drinks too much; it bit her in the ass. Tough* ta-noogies *on her.*

Even empathetic Dash would nix what Jacey was about to do.

She whipped out her cell phone. "Desi, I need you in the Ladies' right now—don't ask why."

Desi must have been right outside the door, because she was there in seconds, asking, "Why?"

"Guard the door," Jacey said. "Do *not* let anyone in."

"Why?"

"Just do it. I'll explain later."

Loyal soldier Desi would cooperate. She always did. Next, Jacey texted Dash and Ivy, who were surely back in their seats by now: *Get Matt, Sierra, and Carlin, and come FAST to the Ladies'. Don't ask why.*

For the second time in less than an hour, she found herself praying for an instant response.

She got her wish. They'd both texted, *WHY?* But they said they'd come.

Meanwhile, Jacey soaked a hand towel in cold water and pressed it to Kate's forehead. "Come on, Kate, you've got to wake all the way up."

"I *wuz* havin' a *mmmm* . . . sweet dream." She hiccuped again.

"No time for dreams now. You have to get up."

Kate didn't move. Jacey crouched and tugged Kate's heels off. Barefoot was the only way. She hooked her arms under Kate's shoulders and tried to pull the girl up. Luckily, Kate was a lightweight, and fit Jacey had no problem getting her vertical.

Now all she had to do was turn Kate around and dunk her head in the sink. It was awkward. Holding her up while briefly immersing her face in the cold water–filled sink was the plan. The goal was to sober her up by shocking her. Instead, Jacey ended up soaking them both.

Meanwhile, Kate spit out the water and babbled incoherently. She was so out of it.

"You won!" Jacey told her. "You won the Teen Choice Award."

"Mmmm . . ." Kate mumbled. Then, shakily, she grasped the sink and tried to pull herself upright without help. Her head lolled. "You're a nice person, Assy. I shouldn't . . . *hiccup* . . . call you that anymore. Assy, not Jacey. 'Cause Sierra *sez* you have a big ass . . . but I . . ."

Jacey dunked Kate's head in the sink again and held it under just a tad longer than necessary.

Finally, after what seemed an eternity but was probably less than ten minutes, Dash, Ivy, and Sierra came blasting into the bathroom, calling out to her.

"Around here, by the wheelchair-accessible stall," she said.

They rounded the curve, and, nearly in unison, slapped their hands over their open mouths—three sets of eyes opened wide in astonishment.

Jacey didn't let them get a word—let alone a question—in edgewise. "Is Matt here? What about Carlin?"

They told Jacey and Desi that Matt was outside the door; Ivy was afraid to let him in without knowing what Jacey's emergency was. Carlin hadn't answered her phone.

Jacey hadn't wanted to execute her hastily dreamed-up plan without Carlin, but there wasn't time to wait. The show would be ending soon. Hundreds of people would pour into the lobby, and dozens of women would be heading for the bathroom.

Jacey directed her friends to stay with Kate in the bathroom while she had a word with Matt.

In seconds, she was back, with these orders: "Wait five minutes. Then, cover Kate's head with a jacket or something, and get her out the back door. A car is waiting. Sierra, you stuff her inside and get her home. Make sure nobody sees you."

"But there's paparazzi surrounding the building," Sierra, who'd sobered up, cried. "There's no way they won't see us."

"Way," Jacey assured her, and ducked into the lobby.

Matt was leaning against the wall, his arms crossed, looking amused.

Jacey tried to ignore that. "Ready?" she asked.

"Sure thing," he said, "but I hope you know what you're doing."

She didn't. But this was the first and only plan that had come to her. And she had no time to wait for another brainstorm.

Matt slung his arm around Jacey's shoulders; she snuggled into him and wrapped her arm around his waist. They walked to the front doors of the theater. Once outside, she tilted her head up to him, and he kissed her. She pressed against him and opened her mouth.

I'm playing a role, she told herself. This isn't real.

A shock of excitement shot through the group of cameramen camped outside the theater. The flashbulb frenzy was fast and fierce. Within seconds, the shutterbug assault was full-on. "Jacey!" "Matt!" "Look here!" "Over here!" "Are you back together?" "Where's Adam?" "What about Carlin?"

Jacey batted her eyelashes and gave the photogs a look of pure surprise.

Matt played his part to the hilt. He held his palm out as if to block their view. "Lay off!" he growled at them. Then he cupped her face, stroked her hair, and gazed into her eyes, as if to show that the media couldn't stop their PDA.

She gazed right back at him. If the eyes were truly the windows to the soul, Matt's soul went deep. God, she was so into him—what was she doing?

He nuzzled her neck and murmured, "You're amazing, Dimples." If this was going to go on much longer—and it had to go on for at least another few moments—Jacey was gonna lose it.

"Right back atcha," she croaked as, entwined, they pretended to make their way toward the valet to get Matt's car.

The whirring of the cameras grew more intense. So did their kisses. It got harder and harder for Jacey to convince herself that this was acting. 'Cause it didn't feel that way at all. It felt so real, so right. She forced herself to count, "one–one thousand, two–one thousand," to calculate how much time their staged make-out session would need. A part of her never wanted it to end; another part wished it'd never begun.

She pulled away from him just slightly. Matt understood. Time to proceed to his car—still kissing and caressing—knowing they'd be trailed. The paparazzi would jump into their own cars and follow them.

And no one would ever know that Dash, Ivy, and Sierra had spirited a wasted Kate out the back door.

Chapter Eighteen

So Robbed!

"Well *that* scene was awardworthy," Matt cracked, expertly steering them through a winding maze of backstreets, pretending they were trying to lose the paparazzi.

"I really appreciate what you did back there. It was very cool," said Jacey, still reeling from the kisses, but managing to keep her composure.

"My pleasure. My unexpected pleasure. You're unpredictable, Dimples, I'll give you that."

She let out a deep sigh of relief, the first one since she'd come across Kate in the bathroom.

"It was really. . . great of you," she stammered stupidly, "on such short notice . . ."

"Imagine what we could have done if we'd had time to

prepare," he said, teasing her.

Matt took one hand off the steering wheel and placed it over hers. "Making out with you wasn't so terrible, Jacey. Even on short notice."

"It was for Kate. *It didn't mean anything.*"

Jacey's phone rang. Dash reported, "Mission accomplished. No one saw us. By the time we got out, all we could hear was the riot you and Matt incited."

"Great. That's great, Dash."

"For who?" Dash challenged. "Who was it great for? Not you—this one's gonna come back to bite you."

Ivy suddenly chimed in, "You've got a lot of 'splainin' to do, little cousin. And it'd better be good."

"I know," Jacey said weakly. "We just have to get through the afterparty."

Matt shot her a sidelong glance. "You really gonna go? That's above and beyond the call of duty."

"Cinnamon would want me to show everyone I'm cool with losing. And, in light of Kate's little stunt, I kind of agree. If only for appearances."

Stopped at a traffic light, Matt turned to her, his eyebrows raised. "Appearances? The one we just staged is gonna land you in the hot seat at the afterparty. It's swarming with press—or did you forget?"

Ooops. In her haste, she'd overlooked that little glitch.

Facing the press right now? Pretty much the last thing she wanted to do. "Good thing I'm an actress," she said.

"Jacey, I—" Matt started.

"I know. You want to talk, Matt. I didn't forget. You did an amazing good deed. But I can't now. I'm just not . . ." She paused, smoothed out her wet, wrinkled top, and noted, "It's been a strange night."

"So you're blowing me off? After I did you this awesome favor?"

"Matt."

"I just want to talk, Jacey. We've got unfinished business, and I'm not cool with it. I don't think you are, either."

Unfinished business? That was how he characterized Carlin, Las Vegas? Not to mention his new squeeze, whoever she was. Wherever she was.

"We need to talk about us—our friendship," Matt said, clarifying matters.

There is no us. That was what she would have said had this been a scene in a movie. His line would have been: *There could be.*

And then, with tears in her eyes, she'd have bravely continued: *Tonight was a onetime thing, signifying nothing.* But she had no script in front of her. She'd been ad-libbing all night.

"We will talk," she finally managed, "after tonight."

Matt surprised her by changing the subject. "Why do you think Kate drank herself into a stupor?"

"She's got a problem?"

"She doesn't think for herself, that's her biggest problem," Matt declared. "From what I hear, she lets herself get led around on a leash; does whatever her manager says. Loses weight, clings to Sierra, plays along with that campaign against you. Accepts roles in movies her manager wants her to do."

Suddenly Jacey remembered Kate's drunken declaration in Las Vegas—was that what she'd meant? Was she apologizing for the anti-Jacey campaign?

"You really think that's why she drinks?"

"You were in a movie with her. Kate's a pretty damned good actress. Or could be. Somewhere deep inside, she knows what she's doing is unhealthy—all of it. But she doesn't have the guts to take matters into her own hands."

"First, I think she needs to be in Betty Ford's hands," Jacey said, "or whatever today's trendy rehab place is."

"Wouldn't know," said Matt with a wink. "I live a clean life."

Now it was her turn to laugh. Yeah, there were a few things about Matt that she was curious about, come to think of it.

★ ★ ★

No way was Matt subjecting himself to the afterparty. It was not his scene. Especially after what they'd just done. He exacted a promise from her to call him, then drove her back to the place where they'd started, at Universal CityWalk. The postshow celebrations were being held on the back-door patio of the theater.

Celebs and their pals were milling about: winners were carrying surfboards, while nonwinners—aka, losers—were pretending to be thrilled anyway; the press, clutching microphones and tape recorders, were there as well. It was the usual suspects: *Access Hollywood*, ET, E!, MTV, *People* magazine, *Us Weekly*, *Teen Vogue*; there were also reps from the online magazines *Teen People* and *Elle Girl*.

She'd have to talk to all of them. And her fallback line, "It was an honor just to be nominated," wasn't gonna cut it tonight. She'd given them much fresher ammunition.

Dash had been deployed as a scout. He saw her alight from Matt's Viper and quickly got her over to the table where Cinnamon, Peyton, Ivy, and Desi were sipping their drinks, waiting for her.

"You're wet—and wrinkled," said Cinnamon, crinkling her nose and pointing to Jacey's formerly sparkly designer top. "And," she sniffed like a pro, "you smell like booze. Where have you been?"

"I'm still damp from a ladies' room mishap, if you can believe that."

"I can't. Nor will anyone else. I don't understand anything you've done tonight. What were you thinking?"

"Honestly, Cinnamon." Jacey turned to include Peyton, "Matt and I just went for a short drive. We only stopped for red lights. We talked, then came straight back here."

The two women both gave her a look that said, "Best find a more believable story, 'cause this one isn't gonna fly."

"If you tell me what really happened, and why, I can make up something credible." Peyton pointed to the not-so-patiently waiting press. "And yes," she said, anticipating Jacey's next question, "you do have to talk to them. Help me help you—that's what you pay me to do."

So, as her friends kept silent, Jacey told Cinnamon and Peyton the truth, showbiz style—that is, just enough of it.

"Matt and me—we were just screwing with the paparazzi. We're not together or anything, it was a total ruse. This way, they think they're getting a hot scoop, which by tomorrow everyone will know was a put-on. It was a blast, beating them at their own game. A little payback."

Cinnamon arched one perfect eyebrow.

"It's true." Ivy backed her up. "I couldn't talk her out of it."

Peyton, always thinking, always spinning, extracted a small bottle of Chanel perfume. "Give me your wrists," she said to Jacey, and proceeded to dab some there and behind her ears to cover up any stinky leftover liquor odor.

"We're all devastated that you didn't win," Cinnamon finally admitted, and Jacey thought she spied a little tear in the corner of her eye. "But really, Jacey, going drinking? I thought you learned your lesson in Las Vegas."

"I'm so completely sober," Jacey assured her, "you have no idea. Even the thought of a drink is pretty nauseating right now."

"However," Desi piped up, "she *is* starving. We all are."

"So are the wolves," Dash said, pointing to the press.

"Okay, on the upside," dictated Peyton, "you're making a positive statement by showing up here. Very meaningful for your image. Without the Matt Canseco factor, there would be no downside at all—especially since Kate wasn't even there. What do you plan to say when they bombard you with questions about Matt?"

"Same thing I told you?" Jacey said doubtfully.

"I'm coming with." Peyton pushed her chair back and stood up. "Brace yourself, Jacey."

They hadn't underestimated the press's interest in Jacey's Canseco Canoodle, as they'd already tagged it.

Every reporter was on it. She pictured them foaming at the mouth and couldn't hide a grin.

"Are you and Matt back together? It looked like you couldn't keep your hands off each other. Care to comment?" The reporter from *Us Weekly* got the jump on the others.

"Looks can be deceiving," Jacey said coyly.

"Not this one," said a second reporter, who held up a camera-phone, showing a steamy photo of them. "This looks very real."

Peyton took a stab at deflecting the line of questions. "I've asked Jacey not to comment on her private life."

An uproar erupted, the gist of which was "She was completely public about it an hour ago—she can't have it both ways."

Jacey tried to suppress a contented smirk. The ruse had worked, big-time. No one believed her excuse about fooling the paparazzi. It was a nonstarter—all were completely invested in this breaking "Hot Couples" news.

In a stroke of good timing, Carlin sashayed by, her tush-length hair swinging, a reminder of her own recent fling with Matt. Which made the faux story all the juicier! Then it hit Jacey that she'd really caught a break when Carlin turned out not to have a role in the Matt scheme. The deceitful beyotch could—and would—have outed everything.

"What about Adam? Does he know he's over?" The E! guy shoved the mic in her face.

She blinked. Adam? Ooops! Her other phony love affair. The phrase "Oh, what a tangled web we weave, when first we practice to deceive" took on special meaning just then.

"Where is Matt now? Why isn't he here with you?" asked *Seventeen*'s reporter.

"Afterparties aren't his scene," she responded smoothly.

She almost kissed the reporter from *Access Hollywood*, who butted in. "The Teen Choice Award is the first thing you ever lost; was Matt consoling you?"

"I also lost prom queen this year," Jacey hadn't realized she was going to say that. "As long as someone deserving wins, I'm cool with it. I didn't need to be consoled."

"Do you think Kate's campaign is the reason she won and not you?" The *Insider* wanted to know.

"I'm not overthinking it. More people voted for her," Jacey said. "She did killer work in *Four Sisters*."

"Do you know why she wasn't there, what really happened?" This was the reporter from *Extra*, but—*sigh*—it wasn't Mark McGrath.

"I know as much as you do," she said convincingly. "Some kind of family emergency."

That wasn't a total lie. It had been an emergency, all right. And, since we're all part of our own families, kind of accurate, in Hollywood-speak, anyway, a language she was getting all too fluent in.

Dash directed the limo driver to In-N-Out Burger, the most famous burger chain in the West. The fast-food joint with the big red sign and bent yellow arrow logo had a very limited menu—and an unlimited following. People drove for miles just to eat their burgers and fries and to down their shakes: they were that good. Those burgers could make a vegetarian think twice, Desi'd declared, more than once.

Of course, everything tasted even better when you were starving, and Jacey's posse hungered for food, and for answers. Happily, the food came first. The foursome squished into a corner table—carrying trays that took up more space than they did! Piled high with In-N-Out Burger's famous Double-Doubles (two cheeseburgers, lettuce, tomato, sauce, and onions on a bun); oodles of greasy, salty fries; and several strawberry, vanilla, and chocolate shakes, they stuffed their faces.

Once the feeding frenzy ended, they were all over Jacey. Questions flew at her from all angles; she did her best to sort, deflect, explain—choosing the easier ones to answer first.

"You wanted Carlin in on this? What were you think-ing?" Ivy demanded.

"Uh . . . brain fart?" Jacey suggested.

"Nope, you had some scene in mind," insisted Dash, who knew her too well. "Give it up."

Jacey took a slurp of her thick chocolate shake. "Everything happened so fast I didn't think it through. But I had this idea that if we came out fighting—me and Carlin—over Matt, it would cause an even bigger uproar."

"That seals it. You're officially insane," said Ivy, wiping her hands on a Wet-Nap.

"She didn't answer her phone, which proves there is a God after all," Dash mumbled, his head in his hands.

"You know what?" Desi said thoughtfully after she'd polished off her first Double-Double. "That would have looked so staged. No one would have bought it."

"How painful was it, kissing Matt?" Ivy now asked, her eyes full of empathy.

You mean putting on an act that really wasn't an act? Pretty painful. Especially now that it's over. Is there such a thing as postpretend depression? Jacey pondered.

"And for what?" Dash asked. "You and Kate were fast friends in Vegas, but really, Jacey—why? Why would you go to such lengths for Kate Summers? Enlighten us, 'cause the three of us are totally in the dark here."

Jacey slumped in her seat and tried to explain, as best she could. "She's not . . . I don't like her, we're not friends. But when I found her there, I knew exactly what would happen if I did nothing. She'd be ripped to shreds by every newspaper, magazine and blog in the country. She'd be so exposed and so hurt. And . . ." She gathered steam as she went on. "I know what that feels like, to some extent. No one deserves to be attacked like that."

"'Cause among tabloid bait, it's all for one, and one for all? Some kind of secret pact? Jacey takes a bullet for the team? Do you even realize how ridiculous that sounds?" Dash blurted out, his frustration finally showing.

"If you were going to create a paparazzi diversion," Ivy said, "why not just use Adam?"

"It was time to stop doing that," Jacey explained. "He came on to me backstage. Remember? I texted you. I would have staged a lip-lock scene that would have been real for him."

"You don't have to confess to us," Ivy said, "but you should admit it to yourself. You wanted to do that scene with Matt."

"Only he didn't do his lines," she mumbled.

"And he never will," Dash said, covering her hand with his. "You're gonna keep hurting yourself—flirting with heartache. I never knew you were a masochist."

Jacey slipped her hand out from under Dash's and pressed her lips together. "I owe you guys big-time for helping me do this. Especially since it seems all of you disapprove. But . . ." She paused and put her fingers together. ". . . But at the end of the day, I shielded Kate because it was the right thing to do."

Dash and Desi understood.

Ivy? Not so much.

"What's up with you?" she demanded. "When did you develop a hero complex? And, if you're so hell-bent on saving sloshed starlets, why not at least get paid for it? If you want to play superhero, you can take that offer."

Jacey lowered her head and stared at the tabletop.

"Is this really the time to bring that up?" Desi challenged Ivy. "This night has been exhausting enough, don't you think?"

"It's hardly coming up for the first time." Ivy retorted.

"In that case," Desi said, turning to Jacey, "for what it's worth, I've been thinking about you playing those kinds of roles."

Three pairs of eyebrows arched. "You have?"

"I know you're worried," Desi went on, "but superheroes aren't just cardboard characters who fly and save the world. They're not perfect, they have inner demons, and they struggle with the duality of their characters: being a human being, and being a hero. If anyone could show how hard that is on-screen, you could."

"Someone's been watching too many episodes of *Heroes*," Dash quipped.

Don't you all see? Jacey wanted to shout. *If I do this, we can say good-bye to life as we know it. Quasi fame, with fans here and there, will give way to body-guards—we won't even be able to do In-N-Out Burger, just the four of us without protection. Forget about going shopping by ourselves! I'll have to endure end-less meetings with media advisers, image consultants, a team of publicists, all telling me what to do, plus a boss dictating what movies I make. What if I let myself be led around like that? What if I turn into Kate?*

It took her a minute to realize no one was speaking. They were all looking at her.

"Like you said, this has been brewing for a long time. Can it wait a couple more days? We'll talk seriously. Promise," Jacey said.

That was two promises she'd made in one night. Neither of which she really wanted to keep.

jaceyfan blog
★ ★ ★ SPECIAL EDITION ★ ★ ★

Sore Loser! Heartbreaker!

What happened? Everyone was so sure the prize was in the bag. Everyone thought Jacey had it locked down. 'Cause who's more famous than our Jace-face? But when all the votes were tabulated— it was the come-from-behind kid, Kate Summers, who jumped in front of Jacey to snag the surfboard. The loss was staggering—but, really, was it any excuse for what happened next? You be the judge.

Another Canseco Canoodle!

Jacey just had to steal the spotlight from the victors. How else to interpret her beyond-diva move? Attention-hog Jacey found a way to trump everyone else's moment of glory. Did she think no one would write about the fact that she *lost* if she got photographed practically making it with Matt Canseco on the red carpet? Did she think no one would pay attention to Kate's shining win? That everyone would be too distracted to pity poor Kate—denied

255

her onstage moment because of a family crisis?

Here's how I see it: Kate put family ahead of fame. That's something Jacey ought to think about. If not family, then, how about another person's feelings? Or did she think it was okay to trample all over nice-guy Adam Pratt's ego, to let him know he's out of the picture by getting her picture in every newspaper and magazine in America with—and I do mean "with"—Matt Canseco? That public display of passion should have been private.

Poor Adam. When reached for comment on Jacey's betrayal, he was too devastated to comment.

P.S.: Jacey, if you think that public service announcement you did reminding kids not to drink and drive is a fix for your image, think again. As you would say, "Not. So. Much."

Chapter Nineteen

No Good Deed Goes Unpunished

Jacey was under attack. Immediately after the Teen Choice Awards, a hailstorm of criticism rained down on her. She was accused of being everything from a spotlight-thief to a boyfriend-humiliating brat to a spiteful sore loser who couldn't accept her opponent's triumph.

Her outfit was torn to tabloid shreds, and her hair was declared a follicular disaster. Even the shape of her eyebrows was criticized.

"And who chose that nail color?" sniped Cojo.

More than the Vegas debacle, the scene at the Teen Choice Awards sent Jacey's popularity spiraling downward, along with her once-wholesome image. She'd been kicked off countless MySpace friends' lists; YouTube was playing her Vegas drunken dance and the Matt make-out session on simultaneous loops. In all, the Jacey-O-Meter was in dangerously dark territory, and she was sure her Q-Score was at an all-time low.

No one except her closest friends suspected the real reason Kate had gone missing at the awards show. No one but those directly involved knew the lengths to which Jacey had gone to protect her rival. And even those people didn't understand why she'd done it. Friends go to great lengths for each other—but putting yourself in the line of fire for a rival? Who would do that? Certainly no one in showbiz. How much more un-Hollywood could you get?

Jacey took perverse pleasure in all this. A sense of satisfaction helped her step around the gossipy land mines that were ready to explode in her face.

There was this, too: in a twisted way, fending off the attacks meant that she didn't dwell on that other event on awards night: losing the Choice Breakout award to Kate.

Despite her worthiness, the teens of America had decided their favorite female breakout star was . . . not her. Everything that'd seemed so critical in the days leading up to the show—her nail color, where she sat, her route to the stage, and who she would hug and thank along the way—ended up completely moot (or, *mute*, as Desi would have said). In a final ironic twist, her acceptance speech had been attributed to someone else.

Okay, she copped to having made that last one happen. Kate and Sierra fell all over themselves thanking Jacey, sending gift baskets and promising to repay the favor, should she ever need it.

So, no regrets, right? Except for the part about getting Matt involved, and the part where she forgot to give Adam a heads-up that she was gonna swap saliva with another guy. Also, the part about bragging that she and Matt had put on a "show" just to mess with the paparazzi. Outraged cameramen all over L.A. had sworn to exact vengeance.

Nearly a week had passed since the awards. Jacey could no longer ignore her disappointment at not winning. It was like a virus spreading unchecked. And it sucked.

Deal with it, her mother would have said. Deal, and get over it, her stepdad would have seconded.

But wait—was it *her* fault she had expected to win? Everyone had *acted* as if it were in the bag. Her agent, publicist, media adviser, image consultant, hairdresser, and especially her posse were in agreement on this. How could she help losing perspective and buying in to all the hype?

A better question: when had she started to care so much?

Because she did care. Enough to feel secret tears

come to her eyes when she watched Kate, now fully recovered, go on TV and chat up her exciting win. Kate, who was glowing while glossing over the family "emergency" that had forced her to leave the awards show early. Kate, busily apologizing for the omission in her acceptance speech: she totally wanted to thank Jacey Chandliss. "For everything."

Jacey cared so much about winning that she felt deserted, abandoned, betrayed, as if fans didn't like her anymore. The girl in the mirror was chubby and short, with a big, round, moony face. A loser. It was as if she were wearing a big, blinking *L* on her forehead.

It wasn't just that. What about her belief that acting itself was the reward? That she needed nothing more than the chance to sink her teeth into a juicy role, to inhabit a character, make a fictional person real to the audience, to be fulfilled? Wasn't that supposed to be enough? Or was that just the way she wanted to see herself?

Blecch. Maybe she wasn't as talented as everyone said she was. Possibly, despite *Generation Next* and those rave reviews for *Four Sisters*, she wasn't so hot after all.Maybe she'd just gotten lucky, and losing the Teen Choice Award had proved that her luck had run out.

'Cause, as Ivy reminded her (not as a criticism): she needed the love. Jacey craved adoration, fed off applause, and basked in the glory of being a star. She lived for it.

If that were true, her decision about taking the big studio offer was a no-brainer. If they still wanted her, that is. If she hadn't screwed it up between the TCA loss, the *Fall from Grace* fiasco, and the spectacle in Las Vegas. What if she'd unhitched herself from the fame train—only no one was brave enough to tell her?

What a colossal joke that would be—on her! All that moaning about selling out, being a puppet of the big studios, bodyguards hovering 24-7, wearing skintight superhero costumes—that whole angsty thing seemed so self-indulgent and adolescent now. Because if the offer had been rescinded, really, where would she be? She'd have to start over and go out for auditions the way every other working actor in L.A. did. And she'd . . . *win some*. And lose some.

Damn Matt Canseco. She hated herself for falling for him and all the "wisdom" he spouted. How could she have been so gullible? Taking everything he'd said as gospel—and acting on it, instead of listening to the people who really had her best interests at heart? To Cinnamon, for example, who'd said it was too soon for her soul. To Ivy, who'd said real stardom was earned.

It had never been in Jacey's nature to be depressed. This was probably the closest she'd ever come. How to extract herself from pity city? There was only one way that she knew of—reaching out to someone who just might be hurting more than she was.

The call to Adam was a long and curious one. She had to let him in on the big secret, the reason she'd made out with Matt. She had to trust that he wouldn't betray her, and Kate's, secret.

She only lied a little—even so, she didn't get away with it. When Jacey explained why she hadn't chosen him as a paparazzi diversion ("they already think we're hooking up, it wouldn't have been a scandal"), Adam—showing powers of perception she never knew he had—responded, "Plus, you didn't want to make out with me—not after I told you how I felt backstage."

Jacey had to cop to it.

Then a weird thing happened. Adam thanked her!

"In the press, I come off as the lover scorned, the naive guy who got humiliated in public. Do you know how great that is for my dating life? How much publicity I'm getting? My agent says I've started to get movie and TV offers, too. People are starting to know my name. It's really cool."

After she hung up, she tried to think up the right cliché for Adam. Zebras never change their stripes? Once a publicity hound, always an attention-grabber? He had gotten over her so quickly that his feelings could never have run that deeply. Still waters ran deep, but Adam was all ripply surface.

Whatever. Talking to Adam had made her feel better.

Too bad the next thing she did brought her right back down. And it was her own fault, again.

The talk in the beach house the next evening centered around Carlin, who'd actually booked a stand-up gig at the famous comedy club the Improv. She was calling it Blond Reasoning ("totally stolen from Jessica Simpson," huffed Ivy), and it was getting a fair amount of advance publicity.

The *Generation Next* people had a stake in her success; they'd paid to get the word out. Plus, they were all flying in to support her. Kia had managed to round up some industry people and friends (who knew she had any?) to fill the audience.

No one in Jacey's inner circle would even have mentioned it, let alone decide to go see it, except for this: rumor had it that Carlin's act took jabs at Jacey—swipes that were thinly disguised as jokes.

Like her friends would let *that* go by.

"One word outta that jealous *beyotch*'s piehole, the skank is toast," threatened Desi, fists in the air.

Ivy advocated heckling, while Dash thought that booing an entire section of her routine would pack more punch. More than enough FOJs (friends of Jacey's) heeded the call. There would be the posse plus Aja, Emilio, Mike, Rob, Gina, Kate, and Sierra—and maybe Matt, depending on his mood.

Jacey was, needless to say, banned from attending. Part of her wanted to go—out of curiosity—but Jacey promised her friends she'd stay far away. Go to a movie. Hang out with Adam. Rent a DVD and eat ice cream.

She lied, but not on purpose.

The night of Carlin's Improv gig, Jacey did start out for the movies. The new Pedro Almodovar flick, which no one in the posse wanted to see, was playing at a nearby cinema in Malibu. She bought a ticket, made her way into the darkened theater, and took a seat on the aisle. She made it through about forty-five minutes (counting the trailers).

Then she called a car service and went to the Improv.

Carlin had not gone on yet, so the timing was perfect—or awful— depending on how you looked at it. Jacey declined to be seated, insisting instead on standing in the shadows at the back of the club, where no one would see her.

Carlin's entrance was accompanied by the kind of loud, lewd whistling men do when they're pumped about what a girl is wearing. Not much, was the deal here. Carlin's tush-length hair was longer than her dress. Her heels were higher than her IQ, Jacey caught herself thinking, especially after her first "joke," which went something like this: "I am so happy to be here. I'm a virgin, you know." She paused for the crowd reaction, which was basically more whistling, and offers to bed her.

"I've never done it . . ." she went on, ". . . in front of such a big audience." Carlin suddenly looked shocked. "I meant, I've never done a stand-up act in such a famous club before! Did you think I meant something else?"

Scattered guffaws followed. That was when Jacey thought, Carlin had best come up with stronger material than that. What followed were her semiamusing takes on life in Cleveland vs. life in Los Angeles. She compared Cleveland's Rock and Roll Hall of Fame with L.A.'s "Walk of Shame." "Back home", Carlin said, "Lake Erie is a place; out here it'd be a horror movie, *Lake Eerie*."

Embarrassed chuckles came from the audience.

Realizing she was bombing, Carlin took aim at Jacey. "Of course you all know me, because I was the runner-up on *Generation Next*." She waited for applause that didn't come. "I came in second to . . . What's her name again?" Carlin pretended to think. "Was it the girl who won last weekend's Teen Choice Awards? No, not her."

Jacey felt a sharp stab. Why had she come?

Meanwhile, the posse started a low hissing in the background.

Carlin continued. "I'm kidding! Everyone knows the winner of *Generation Next* was Jacey Chandliss. And she was robbed of that Teen Choice Award."

That got her some real applause, and Jacey felt a little better. But not for long.

"I came out here as Jacey's guest, and I'm so grateful to her," Carlin gushed. "Everything I know about showbiz, I learned from her. All the tricks of the trade."

Jacey braced. *Here it comes. Let's see what she's got.*

"Jacey taught me how to act like a star." Shockingly, Carlin had a picture of the Slickity Jeans ad, enlarged and projected on the wall behind her.

"See," she said, pointing, "that's Jacey in front, with little tiny ol' me stuck way in the back. Jacey taught me all about airbrushing. It's a special effect to make you look thinner. See?"

Suddenly, the screen split in half. A "real" picture of Jacey—an awful paparazzi shot in which she looked like a heifer—was side by side with the magazine picture. The posse began to boo.

Carlin continued.

"Jacey taught me how to live in Hollywood before you have a job or any money." The next slide was a picture of Jacey's beach house, juxtaposed with a tiny, shacklike cottage, presumably Kia's house. "I'm sure it's 'cause she

266

wanted me to learn humility that she kicked me out."

Desi heckled, "You deserved it, bitch!"

"Oh, I'm kiddin'! I see all of Jacey's friends in the audience—hey, as long as you paid the admission, I'm glad you came. Unlike your boss, I need the money! See, here's another secret Jacey taught me: how to get everything you need, and everything you want, for free!"

Over the hoots of Jacey's crowd, and with the aid of the pictures projected behind her, Carlin detailed all the designer fashions Jacey wore to various events, all the goodies that had come when she was being wooed to appear in ads.

Kate called out, "You're just jealous!"

"Oh, no, *au contraire*," Carlin responded. "I wouldn't want all this stuff if it meant I'd be a star like Jacey. 'Cause that's when the tabloids expose things that you don't want the world to know! Like this." The magazine headline *Jacey in a Jealous Love Rage* was now projected on the screen. Underneath was a shot of Carlin making out with Matt.

"See, that's kind of true, but how humiliating for her!" Carlin pretended to sound remorseful.

The heckling from the audience had begun in earnest, but Carlin was prepared. "Hey, look, I feel bad for the girl, too. Who wouldn't fall for Matt Canseco's advances?"

Dash, Aja, and Emilio were now holding Desi and Ivy back from storming the stage, which allowed Carlin to continue. "But here's the thing I am most grateful for. I want to thank you, Jacey, for moving over. You were once the hottest new star in Hollywood, but now? You couldn't even snag a Teen Choice Award. Shouldn't that tell you something? 'Cause this is my time to shine! Like I said, Jacey is just so generous! I could not have asked for a better mentor. Or is that . . . *dementor*?!"

Jacey had had enough. Tears streaming down her face, she fled the club, beating herself up for coming.

Chapter Twenty

The Secluded Cove, Part Two

A funny thing happened on the ride home from the *un-funny* comedy club. Still sobbing, Jacey hadn't responded to the limo driver's question about what kind of music she wanted. He'd been tuned in to an oldies station, when a familiar song came on. Through her tears, Jacey broke into a grin. Thanks for rubbing it in, radio station, she thought. It was the ridiculous song Carlin had had them play back at the Slickity Jeans photo shoot: "Lucky," the Britney Spears oldie about the poor little rich starlet who has it all, but cries herself to sleep every night. Jacey couldn't help herself; she started to laugh. Because what was worse than losing to Kate, more humiliating than being vilified by Carlin, was that she was actually in danger of becoming a cliché!

By the time the limo dropped her off at her Malibu pad, she was done laughing at herself, and finished with feeling sorry for herself. She just felt empty.

That was a feeling that didn't have staying power. Tomorrow, she'd be fine. But for now, on this starlit Malibu night in November, she needed the beach. The crescent-shaped stretch of soft white sand right in front of her house would do just fine. From the moment she'd decamped there back in August, being in Malibu had made her feel healthy and optimistic, as if new opportunities stretched before her, limitless as the horizon. Maybe it was a spiritual thing.

Jacey ducked into her room to kick off her shoes and grab a sweatshirt, blanket, flashlight, and bottle of water. She tossed her designer bag, Sidekick, and phone on the bed and left them there.

There was no way she wasn't going to the cove. Before Carlin corrupted it, it'd been her place. What better night to reclaim it, if only symbolically?

After she walked to the beach, Jacey deliberately spread her blanket out on the spot where she estimated Matt and Carlin had been. She plopped her butt down on it, hugged her knees, and filled her lungs with salt air. She marveled once again at how a girl who'd grown up per-fectly happy in a landlocked suburban subdivision had come to feel so alive by the ocean.

She'd been a sheltered sixteen-year-old when the *Generation Next* express had rolled into her life. She'd been a high school kid full of ideals, dreams, and, not to put too fine a point on it, plans, about the way her life would play out. She'd go to college as a film major, star in theater, and be recruited, most likely, by a Hollywood scout, or someone important. In her daydreams, she was never exactly sure how she ended up a star, just that she did.

Love had seemed clearer. She had figured she would spend forever with Logan; she had hoped that forever would start on prom night, the night she'd chosen to make love to him for the first time.

That hadn't worked out so well. The breakup was painful, but from this distance, she gave props to Logan for honesty.

Adam had operated similarly. He'd put it out there, admitting, without prodding, that he wanted to use her to make himself famous. And when he discovered he was really into her, he told her that, too.

She'd hurt Logan by choosing Hollywood over him; she'd bruised Adam by turning him down.

So maybe it was just that the karma gods had spoken, that the guy she was crazy about made it complicated, vague, and messy. Holding her so tight she felt a part of him, but then pulling away; kissing her passionately, but then doing the tongue tango with someone else; telling her he couldn't be with her, but then stroking her arm, running his fingers through her hair, and finally leaving Las Vegas with a new girlfriend. Causing a meltdown inside her body every time she saw him.

The one thing she wanted most from him—which was himself—was the one thing he wouldn't give. Was that her penance for getting everything; for living her dream; for being the It girl, the rich girl, the beauty, with friends who always had her back—you had to pay some way, right?

So maybe, this was—new-word alert—her *mazel*. Her luck.

How to turn that around? Give it up, go back to Michigan. Would life even out then? Would she find true love?

Idly, she picked up a stray twig and began to doodle in the sand. She drew a heart. Then she drew a zigzag line cutting through it: a broken heart. In one half she wrote her name. In the other, she fitted Logan's, Adam's, Matt's. She'd just finished her masterpiece when she heard footsteps. Who dared trespass on her territory?

Her heart flew as he came into view. Why was he doing this?

Matt was fully dressed, in loose-fitting jeans, tight black T-shirt, and motorcycle boots. She didn't trust herself to speak.

He waited until he was almost upon her, then nodded at her beach blanket. "Is this spot taken?"

"What are you doing here, Matt?"

"You didn't call—you said you would—I had to hunt you down," he said, settling down next to her.

"I was going to," she fibbed. "I just needed to figure some stuff out."

"Fair enough," he said. "Anyway, in case no one's texted or called you yet, I thought I'd fill you in on Carlin's act." The mention of her name, coming from him, nauseated her.

"Don't bother." Jacey shook her head. "I was there."

"You were? I didn't see you." He seemed shocked.

"I didn't see you, either." She *was* shocked.

"I dunno why I went. Curiosity, plus everyone else was there. I couldn't bring myself to be in the audience, so I stood in the back," he admitted.

"Me, too!" They must have been on opposite sides of the club, oblivious of each other.

"So then you know!" he said cheerily. "I don't need to tell you."

"That she trashed me? Yeah, that was fun."

Matt looked at her curiously. "Wait a minute—when did you leave?"

"I don't remember; she was tearing me down; I wasn't looking at the clock."

"So you *don't* know, then," he said with satisfaction. "Carlin McClusky got her true comeuppance, in just the way that would hurt her most."

"My posse heckled her?" Jacey guessed. "Kate threw rotten tomatoes? What?"

"No one laughed. After a few polite heh-heh-heh's in the beginning, the room went dead silent. Your friends didn't have to do anything; she did it to herself. She wasn't funny. She tanked."

Wow, Jacey thought, karma rocks!

Matt continued, "Not that it makes up for what she did. Or the lies she spread about you. You have no idea how many times I wanted to call up *Access Hollywood* or some Web site and tell them what a good person you are, what you did for someone else, without any recognition."

Jacey was silent for a moment.

"You would have done the same thing, right, Matt? If someone you knew was about to be tarred and feathered. You would've found a way to divert the press's attention." Jacey hadn't realized she was going to say that.

"No question. My instinct would definitely be to keep

someone out of a surefire scandal, the kind that the press would feed on for weeks. But that's not the only reason I agreed to help you." He covered her hand with his. Her sand heart caught his attention, and he gently took the twig and crossed out his name.

"It's not?"

"No. And that's what I was trying to tell you. When I saw you backstage, I realized something, and I tried to say it, but you weren't having it. Later, when we were alone in the car, making our getaway, you didn't want to hear it. So I'm asking you—would now be a good time?"

"Take your best shot." Jacey tried to sound casual, but she couldn't keep a smile from starting to spread across her face. He knew how to make her laugh and how to push her buttons every single time.

Suddenly, he got nervous, tentative. Nervous didn't come naturally to Matt Canseco. He fidgeted, cleared his throat, couldn't figure out where to look. Finally, he spit it out.

"I am so bummed about the thing with Carlin."

He wasn't talking about the comedy club.

"Letting myself be used by her. She came on to me and—"

Jacey put up her palm, stopping him. "I'm over it. You don't owe me an explanation."

"Right." He exhaled, still edgy. "I don't have to say

anything. And if it'd happened with any other girl, in any other situation, I probably never would have. But I've changed since I've known you. So, please, just listen to me." He started to reach for her.

"Don't touch me, okay? When you do that, it confuses me." That was all Jacey could manage.

"It'll be hard—" he began, almost jokily.

"Don't. Go. There," she warned, and she moved over, putting more space between them.

He took a deep breath. "Here's the thing, Jacey. I know you think I'm a player. A guy who comes on to every pretty girl—like you—then goes on to the next one. I thought it would be okay as long as I was honest with you. "

"How were you honest, Matt?" she asked softly.

"By telling you the truth. I'm crazy-attracted to you—and not just physically. Though that's definitely there," he repeated, looking at her longingly. "I told you I couldn't be with just one person. Certain people are just not built that way; they're incapable of being true to one person. I was one of those people."

Was?

He quickly corrected himself. "*Am* one of those people."

Her face fell; she turned away before he could see it.

"Wait, maybe . . ." he stumbled. "Jacey, I don't know anymore."

Figure it out. Once, he'd said those very words to her. She was tempted to throw them back at him. But this speech, confession, whatever it was, clearly was hard for him.

"All I know is when I saw that look on your face . . . when you saw us . . . It killed me, Jacey. I wanted to die."

I wanted you both to die. Another thought better left unsaid.

"I told myself," he rambled on, "'Nothing's changed. I feel crappy cause I just never wanted to hurt her.' Hurt you. That it wasn't anything, y'know, stronger."

Stronger? Meaning what?

"Anyway, after it happened—the thing with Carlin— I let myself be talked into what our friends were saying. I stopped trying to talk to you. Trying to see you."

"And then we found ourselves in Las Vegas," she said, knowing what was coming next.

"It hurt so much—watching you—I knew exactly how you were feeling, why you were acting crazy like that. I wanted to take you aside, make you stop, but . . ."

"You had all those girls on your lap, so you couldn't get up." It came out of Jacey more snarky than she had intended.

"Hey, you weren't the only one who had too much to drink that night. I was pretty smashed, and when that happens, I can do crazy things. So, like an idiot, I did nothing."

"You left," she reminded him. "I'll never forget that look on your face. It crushed me. You were revolted. Disgusted."

"With myself, Jacey, not with *you*! For letting things get out of hand. Being my stupid self, I took it out on the hotel, on everyone who crossed my path. I acted as lamely as you did."

"Lamely, but not lonely. I left with a hangover; you managed to leave with a beautiful girl on your arm," Jacey pointed out.

"A girl? What girl?" Matt seemed sincerely flummoxed.

"'The brunette with the never-ending legs,' is what the tabloids are calling her. Ring a bell?"

"My cousin Susie? She lives in Vegas, I gave her a ride to L.A.—Jacey! You of all people, believe that stuff? How is that even remotely possible? All you had to do was ask Emilio; he'd have set you straight."

"I didn't want to ask. Not then. I just assumed."

"You know what happens when you assume," he said, moving close to her, and whispering in her ear. "You make an ass . . . out of *U* and me."

She wanted to laugh, but her heart was pounding. She was so drawn to him; she so wanted to be with him, to touch him, to fall into him. Matt pulled her into his arms and held her close. She could hear and feel his heart thumping, just as *rat-a-tat-tat* as hers was. He was stroking her hair, murmuring, holding her tight. Her arms found their way around his neck.

She raised her head, just enough to look at him: his strong chin, his smooth cheeks, those mesmerizing eyes. Those lips, now just brushing hers.

When they opened their mouths, when they kissed, when he cradled her face, when they pressed into each other passionately, it was different from doing it in front of an audience of paparazzi. Completely, devastatingly different.

Don't let this end, went the loop playing in her brain.

"Wait, I wasn't finished." He struggled to catch his breath.

Me, either.

He cupped her chin, gazed into her eyes. His words came more easily now. "If you're okay with this, I'd like to try . . . you and me. A relationship where I—where we—don't see anyone else."

Jacey's stomach somersaulted, and she began to tremble. "Please, Matt, don't say that because you feel guilty, because you don't want to hurt me—"

"It's because I can't keep you off my mind, Dimples.

Because you just wormed your way into my heart. Because . . . you're you. And . . ." He picked up the twig she'd been drawing with and drew his own heart shape in the sand. "I heart you."

"I'm seventeen—" she whispered when they came up for air. "Not too young anymore?"

"Almost eighteen," he murmured. "Almost legal."

"If you change your mind, if you want to see other people, promise you'll tell me; don't go behind my back." Who knew you could kiss and talk at the same time?

"Only if you promise, too." His voice was husky, hushed.

And with the waves crashing by their side, they sealed the deal.

jaceyfan blog

Fiesta, Fiesta

I hear Jacey's throwing a party. I hear a very select
few are invited. I'm not one of them. There's a good
reason for that—she still has no clue who I am! Slap
me five, I am *that* good.

Chapter Twenty-One

Everyone Who's Anyone

An intimate gathering with
Jacey Chandliss & friends.

WHERE: Jacey's joint in Malibu

WHEN: Sunday around 4-ish

DON'T BYO: Bling, fake-bakes, or egos

PLEASE DO BYO: Frizzy hair and flip-flops,
and your appetite!

WHO'LL BE THERE: Everyone who's anyone.

This REALLY means you!

The catering truck was parked in the driveway. Dash and
Ivy were helping the waitstaff set up hors d'oeuvres and

drinks on the deck. They'd ordered fun finger foods, like pigs in a blanket, deviled eggs, buffalo wings, guacamole, nachos, chips, cheese and crackers, and all kinds of fattening dips. And, in a nod to Cinnamon, a plate of raw veggies.

No caviar, overpriced sushi, undercooked meat, nor ochazuke like what she'd had at the last party. Today, the rule was, if Desi couldn't pronounce it, they weren't having it.

Around sunset, Jacey planned to have a bonfire on the beach, roast marshmallows, and tell ghost stories. Or, in this case, Hollywood stories, the kind that really set spines tingling, because they were real.

Only the most elite VIPs had been invited, and they had been asked to keep it on the down-low. Translation: no celebutantes, rockers, hip-hoppers, heiresses, scions, or studio heads. And no one (aside from Jacey, of course) who appeared in *US Weekly*, *In Touch* or any other tabs on a daily basis.

To make this guest list there was only one requirement: you had to count in Jacey's world. Everyone was a someone because, unlike the scene at her wrap party, everyone here could be trusted. Each had a special place in her heart. She'd invited them all here on the Sunday prior to Thanksgiving because she had a few announcements.

And because, truly, she was thankful.

"Hey, you." Ivy tapped her on the shoulder. "Come take a walk with me."

"Now? Everyone will be here soon," Jacey said.

"Exactly. I want to talk to you before they arrive."

Mmmm . . . what could this mean? Jacey surveyed the scene. Dash was supervising the caterers; Desi and Mike were in charge of setting up the campfire down by the shoreline. Ivy had finished putting out the drinks. Everything was on track. There really was no reason she couldn't take a walk with Ivy. Except for the fact that Ivy might have bad news. That'd be scary.

They headed north along the shore, toward the Paradise Cove Beach Café.

"So, what's up?" They were only a few yards from the house, but Jacey was too nervous to wait.

"I have a confession. It's best if you know now, before anyone gets here," Ivy told her.

Jacey tensed. All kinds of scenarios flashed through her mind. Was Ivy leaving? Was Ivy engaged to Emilio? Had Ivy taken another job? Had she—what?

"I did something behind your back." Ivy filled in the blank, continuing her long, graceful strides, not looking at Jacey.

"What did you do, Ives—am I going to freak out?"

"I hope not, and I hope you understand I did it with your best interests at heart."

"I trust you, Ives. Just spill it."

Ivy took a deep breath. "I told Cinnamon—in total confidence—what really went down the night of the Teen Choice Awards. Why you skipped out early, made out with Matt in front of the cameras, and came back disheveled, and you know, smelly."

"I don't understand why you did that."

"Because after the paparazzi frenzy, Landsman took the offer back. Said he'd changed his mind, that you had sullied your image one too many times—"

"I didn't win, that's the real reason," Jacey interjected. "He doesn't want to be associated with a loser."

"He doesn't see you that way. When I told Cinnamon, she picked up the phone and called him. She pitched you as a hero! The sweetest, most unselfish, wholesome hero, who acted in someone else's best interests at the cost of her own. Trust me, Jace, that never happens in Hollywood! Anyway, he bought it—he wants you more than ever. He's even sweetened the deal. Only, don't say anything to anyone, because no one knows that Cinnamon knows. And Cinnamon doesn't know that I told you that she knows."

"Huh?" Jacey's head was spinning. Only in Hollywood

could things get this twisted but in the end work out okay somehow.

"Now, listen carefully, here's the most important part," said Ivy. "This *doesn't* mean you have to take the deal. I wanted you to have options. Choices. The ball's back in your court. And whatever you decide, we'll all be here to play."

Playing defined Jacey's party. No work, no pretensions, no rivalries, no showbiz crap. No one seemed more eager to catch that vibe than Cinnamon. In what might have been a first in public, the agent wore her lustrous black hair loose, instead of in her usual sleek chignon. She gave Jacey a human hug, making actual contact!

And she *ate* like nobody's business! Real food. Fattening food. Without scooping out the bread, cutting off the crust, pushing away the cheese. Agent-babe stuffed her un-made-up face guilt-free and happily. Jacey was beyond jazzed.

Of course, it wasn't as if Cinnamon had had a full personality transplant. She did find a moment during the party to lean over and declare, "The nominations for the Golden Globes will be out in a couple of months."

Yup, that campaign was already started in Cinnamon's head. No doubt.

Tall, slender Peyton had ditched her tailored Calvin Klein clothes for loose Levis, a tank top, and sneakers. Best of all, there was no tape recorder on her person, and never once did the words *press release* or *spin control* come out of her mouth.

Adam Pratt arrived with Kate and Sierra. He'd ended up getting chummy with them after being at so many events with them and possibly because he now knew the truth about what'd happened back on awards night. (Knowing a secret about someone else makes everyone feel powerful.)

But Jacey didn't think the budding friendship was about that. Could have been he actually felt sorry for Kate, that the former ice queen was now vulnerable in his eyes. Jacey distinctly remembered his *not* taking part in her own drunken debacle, and, instead, trying to extract her from the hot tub.

She wondered, too, if it hadn't been Adam's influence that'd persuaded Kate and Sierra to bring a gift to Jacey. 'Cause it wasn't something that duo would have thought of on their own, she believed.

Jacey's jaw dropped when she saw it. The surfboard! Kate's trophy! "No way," she said, shaking her head. "I couldn't take it. You won it."

"You deserve it," Kate said. "You saved my career."

"Besides," snickered Sierra, nearly back to her old self, "it's not the real one. You couldn't think Kate would part with that one. This is another one we had made for you."

Straight outta the pages of *Duh Magazine*, Jacey thought.

"I fired my manager, McSleazeball," Kate admitted shyly when Sierra turned away to greet Cinnamon and Petyon. "And"—her eyes were downcast— "I'm seriously considering AA."

"That's very cool, Kate," Jacey said encouragingly. "Takes guts."

When Emilio, Aja, Rob, and Matt got there, the party got into full swing.

The mood stayed casual and upbeat. After eating, swilling, and chatting, Matt started a kickball game by the ocean, and everyone, including Cinnamon, was into it. In fact, it was Jacey's agent who suggested the game be boys versus girls. Of course, Cinnamon probably knew that Peyton was a former soccer star. And that actors and play-wrights, even Matt, Adam, and Rob, were not known for their sports prowess. She couldn't have known, however, that tiny Desi was also a power kicker, or that Ivy ran track in college.

With the guys' pride on the line—the idea of losing to girls in kickball was bogus, man—the first game was hard-fought. No one cared about getting wet, messy, or fall-in-the-sand gritty. Not even Sierra, who did okay in the outfield. So, when the girls killed, on the strength of Desi's dynamite kicking "skillz," Matt's team insisted on playing for best two out of three.

Tragically, the boys beat the babes in the end, but not without plans for a rematch.

Later, when everyone had decamped to the deck for nourishment, Matt took Jacey aside and slipped his arm around her waist.

"I have a proposition for you," he said.

"You're proposing? Don't you think it's a little early in our relationship?" she asked, kidding him.

"A proposition. Not a proposal," he clarified. "Anyhow, what do you think about working with me and Rob on a screenplay? Something the three of us could do together, and if we get lucky, maybe even produce and star in?"

Jacey eyes widened.

"Unless you can't, that is, if you decide to go with the superhero offer." Matt had misinterpreted her silence.

"No, no, that won't be a problem," she rushed to assure him. "I'm just surprised you and Rob would think of me as creative. As more than an actress. That's very flattering."

"I'll take that as a yes," Matt said, holding her close and lifting her chin to kiss her.

"We can talk more about it later, and do other things later," Jacey said with a wink, "but the sun's about to go down."

"And?"

"You'll see."

The sunset was spectacular. Jacey could not have ordered up a better one had she scripted it. The setting sun was a big round ball, just balancing on the straight line the horizon formed, casting a pink light against the navy-colored ocean.

She invited all her guests to sit around the campfire down by the shore and gave out beach blankets and towels. Mike was in charge of keeping the fire going, while Desi distributed long skewers and Ivy passed around bags of marshmallows.

As the roasting began, Dash and Aja hauled down buckets of beer, wine, water, and soda.

Soon, the sun would dip down below the horizon. Then they'd have just the fire and the moonlight to see by. Jacey was the only one with something to read, but she'd memorized what she was going to say.

Finally, she stood up and asked for everyone's attention. "I have an announcement and a favor to ask. Also a speech to read."

"All that?" Emilio pretended to be miffed. "How long

did you think we were gonna sit here?"

"You have somewhere else to be?" Ivy elbowed him playfully.

Jacey took a deep breath. "Okay, first my announcement: after much consideration, and feet-dragging, obsessing, and definitely overanalyzing—*and* at the risk of alienating some of the people I admire and adore and believe in and trust—I've decided to—" She paused for effect. She was, after all, an actress.

"—Take the offer." Jacey said finally. "I'll play superheroes. Hopefully I'll do it well enough that, as Desi hopes, they won't be cardboard characters, but fleshed out, complex, and relatable."

Cinnamon's jaw dropped. Her skewer and marshmallow followed, landing in the fire.

Ivy jumped up, tears in her eyes. "We'll make it good, Cousin, you won't regret it." She hugged her.

"There are, however, some conditions," Jacey added when Ivy sat back down. "If possible, I would like it in the contract that I will be allowed to appear in smaller, independent films, or plays, or parts on TV, between each big-box-office movie I make."

Matt pumped his fist in the air. "That's my Dimples!"

"And I want some of that big paycheck they're giving me to be put aside for good causes. Charitable causes. I'm asking Dash to help me work that out."

"Is that the favor?" Dash wanted to know.

"No. The favor is helping me figure out who the blogger is. We've let him or her get away with a ton of stuff; I think it's time to root him out—or her. I accept being paparazzi bait and trashed in the tabloids, but this guy knows too much, and I've had enough. So the favor is, if we all get with our Nancy Drew and Hardy Boys, put our Rolodexes together . . ." She trailed off, having made her point.

"And now, for my speech!"

"Finally," Rob said. "We've been waiting long enough!"

"The one I would have given at the TCAs was handled, with aplomb, by Sierra. Kate, she'll tell you later what 'aplomb' means. Anyway, I wrote a new one, for a new audience. This time I speak not as the TCA winner, but as the real winner. Indulge me."

"It's all you," said Aja. "Go right ahead."

"It was an honor to be nominated—no bull. Eighteen months ago at this time, in this town, I was a nobody. Eighteen days ago, I was on the short list for a national award. How huge is that? No one here is so jaded we can't remember when we were just regular people, nobodies."

"I'm still a nobody!" Emilio shouted, raising his beer bottle.

"Give it up for the nobodies!" Aja seconded, clinking his bottle against Emilio's.

Jacey giggled. "More recently, I thought it was the most amazing, awesome, surreal thing that I'd given a party, and everyone came. The Hollywood A-list, the hotties, all the boldfaced names. I felt like I was part of this exclusive club. One of them.

"A lot's gone down over the past few months. Not all of it was so great. But a lot of lessons were learned. Like, when you're the It girl, when everyone's on your side, that's easy—everyone's your friend then; everyone wants to be around you. When you screw up, or you lose out or make a total fool of yourself, that's when the A-list takes a powder; they scatter; no one wants to be associated with you. Except the real A-list. My personal A-list."

She took a sharp breath. Everyone's eyes were on her.

"I'd like to thank Cinnamon, for everything you do for me, whether you agree or not. I would not have lasted two days in H'wood with you."

Cinnamon tilted her head, closed her eyes, and whispered, "Thank you."

Jacey turned to her publicist. "I'd like to thank Peyton for your patience, your smarts, your unflappable ability to deal, no matter how much I screw up. Here's my spin on you: you're the best!

"I'd like to thank Adam for a lot of things, but right now, I'll just say, I'm glad our phony romance worked for you!" Adam laughed and clapped.

"I'd like to thank Rob, for your talent, for giving me the opportunity to inhabit such an amazing character."

Rob raised his wine glass. "Back atcha."

"My guys, my posse, my BFFs: Dash, Ivy, and Des. For you guys I have no words. It's all unconditional love between us. So I figured, actions are good, too. I'm selling the house in Beverly Hills. We're staying here, in Malibu."

That was met with cheers and whoops, and, from Desi, hanging on to Mike, a "Yessss!"

"To Emilio, Aja, and Mike: you guys make my friends happy. And that makes me happy. So . . . don't muck it up!"

Everyone laughed.

"And to Matt. Thank you for teaching me, for mentoring me, for opening my world and showing me the endless horizon, what the future could be."

Matt wasn't smiling. He was too busy trying to choke back the lump in his throat, to keep from showing the tears in his eyes.

"It's an honor to know all of you, to call you my friends. If I get too self-absorbed, too big for my not-skinny-size britches, kick my butt. If I get on the wrong track, doing things that are self-destructive, intervene.

"'Cause here's the most important thing Hollywood has taught me. It's not about who can do what for you— it's about who is there for you. And just as importantly, who you are there for. I'm always here for you guys."

"You know what, Dimples?" Matt said, looking at her adoringly, lovingly, and gratefully. "I'll drink to that."

"I thought you might." Jacey raised her own glass. "To us. To the future!"

Acknowledgments

Lots of cool people helped with this book—my own personal "Everyone Who's Anyone" list includes: Helen Perelman, Jennifer Besser, Arianne Lewin, Phyllis Wender, and always, the family and friends.